Aubrey De Vere

The Foray of Queen Meave, and Other Legends of Ireland's Heroic

Age

Aubrey De Vere

The Foray of Queen Meave, and Other Legends of Ireland's Heroic Age

ISBN/EAN: 9783337152710

Printed in Europe, USA, Canada, Australia, Japan

Cover: Foto ©Andreas Hilbeck / pixelio.de

More available books at **www.hansebooks.com**

THE FORAY

OF

QUEEN MEAVE

AND OTHER

LEGENDS OF IRELAND'S HEROIC AGE

BY

AUBREY DE VERE

LONDON
MACMILLAN & CO.
1893

PREFACE.

THE 'Foray of Queen Meave,' the longest of the following poems, is founded on and in substance represents the far-famed 'Tain bo Cuailgné,' a tale regarded by many Irish scholars as the great Irish epic of ancient times, by others as a part only of some larger epic of which numerous portions remain, but which unhappily found no Pisistratus to combine them into a whole. The lamented Professor Eugene O'Curry has expressed his opinion that 'in the time of Senchan and St. Columba' (that is in the sixth century) 'it was generally believed that Fergus was the original writer of the tale.'[1] 'On this supposition it must have existed in a rudimental form a little before the Christian Era. It was lost for several centuries, but recovered in the sixth, when, according to the legend recorded by Professor O'Curry, St. Kiaran wrote down the tale "in a book which he had made from the hide of

[1] *Lectures on the MS. Materials of Ancient Irish History*, p. 41.

his pet cow—a book called the Leabhar na h-Uidré." [1] Elsewhere that great authority states that a large portion of this work is preserved in a copy 'written at the same Clonmacnoise by a famous scribe named Maelmire, who was killed there in 1106.[2] That copy of St. Kiaran's version is still extant in the Royal Irish Academy, as well as a copy of a later version included in the 'Book of Leinster,' a collection compiled about 1150. Translations of both these versions have been made by Professor O'Looney, and to both I have had access through his kindness. These two versions differ much from each other, the earlier being the simpler and stronger, while the later is the richer in detail. To the sixth century belong not a few Irish works of unquestioned authenticity, such as the elegy written by Dallan Forgaill on the death of St. Columba, A.D. 592, found also in the Leabhar na h-Uidré. To an earlier period, the fifth century, belongs the tract entitled the 'Battle of Magh Tuireadh,' or Moytura. Several poems are confidently referred to Dubthach, chief Bard of King Laeghaire, St. Patrick's earliest convert at the Royal Court; and to the same century belongs the Senchas Mor, or Compilation of Laws. The 'Tripartite Life of St. Patrick'

---

[1] *Lectures on the MS. Materials of Ancient Irish History*, p. 30.
[2] *Manners and Customs of the Ancient Irish*, vol. iii. p. 403.

is attributed by Colgan and others to the sixth century, because it mentions as still living many persons known to have died before the close of that age. Books are recorded as having been in the hands of the Druids before St. Patrick's time, or soon after, such as the 'Cuilmenn,' the 'Sailtair of Tara,' attributed to the third century, the 'Book of St. Mochta,' one of St. Patrick's early disciples, the 'Book of Cuana,' &c. There is consequently nothing to surprise us in the circumstance that the 'Tain bo Cuailgné' belongs to a period so early. The following poem, written of course in the character of an old Irish bard, is not a translation except as regards some passages which occur chiefly in Fragment III. It is not in the form of translation that an ancient Irish tale of any considerable length admits of being rendered in poetry. What is needed is to select from the original such portions as are at once the most essential to the story, and the most characteristic, reproducing them in a condensed form, and taking care that the necessary additions bring out the idea, and contain nothing that is not in the spirit, of the original.

An attempt to introduce to modern readers a work so ancient, and connected with allusions so unfamiliar, seems to call for some remarks on the character of that work, and on the age which produced it. The 'Tain bo

Cuailgné' is especially valued, not only for its poetic merits, but for the light which it throws upon early Irish customs, such as the use of the war-chariot, abandoned, apparently, as early as the second century. It marks strikingly the mutual relations of Ireland's different kingdoms, classes, and races. It is the amplest voice from Ireland's 'Heroic Age,' thus belonging to the first, as the so-called 'Ossianic' poems belong to the second cycle of ancient Irish song. The latter cycle derives its name from the circumstance that, though little of it can be traced back to Ossian, it records the warriors of the Fianna Eireann who were his contemporaries, and flourished in the second century. Yet even they, scarcely excepting Diarmid, Oscar, and Fionn himself, though the terror of Ireland's provincial kings till their power, rendered too exacting by long success, was extinguished by a single fatal reverse, were never counted equal to the mighty ones of her earlier time.

The Heroic Age had reached its highest greatness shortly before the Christian Era. It was then that Fergus Mac Roy reigned over Uladh, now Ulster; but he renounced his throne, incensed at seeing his wily stepson preferred to him, and was exiled because he had revenged the murder of Usnach's sons. Among the ancient Irish heroes he was the popular favourite, princely in all his ways, magnanimous, truthful, just, and not the less majestic because a man of mirth. His supplanter, Conor Conchobar, was his opposite in all things, a man more sagacious, but perfidious and implacable. At that time lived also Conal Carnach, and his foster-son Cuchullain immeasurably the greatest of all Ireland's legendary warriors. His character is one so consistent and so original that it suffices by itself to stamp the age which conceived it as high among the most poetic of the world. Cuchullain has been called the Achilles of early Erin; yet with the swiftness, the fierce impulse, and indomitable might that belonged to the Greek, he blends in perfect harmony qualities that remind us more of Hector. Like him, he is the defender of the city, more inspired by patriotic zeal than even by his love of glory: like him, he is generous, modest, forbearing to the weak. It is to the strong only among his country's foes that he is unpitying; and even in his dealings with them there is no ferocity. They have to die, and he slays them. He is reverent to both his parents—fiercely as they were at variance with each other —to age, to woman; and about him, even in his sterner moods, there plays often the joyous spirit of the child. His devotion to Ferdia is tenderer than that of Achilles to Patroclus; but on him there has fallen a sterner duty.

He has not to avenge that friend, but to encounter and lay him low when the invader of Uladh. The one blemish in Cuchullain's life, his desertion of Aifné, his boyhood's love in Scatha's Island, for a rival whose chief attraction was perhaps that she could only be won by force of arms, is an episode not included within the scope of the Tain. His lifelong aspiration was fulfilled. A few years after the repulse of Meave, while the other warriors of Ulster were engaged on an invasion of Alba (Scotland), Cuchullain alone remained behind for the protection of his country. Suddenly the forces of all the other kingdoms fell again upon the northern land, stirred up by ancient hatred, and led on by a remnant of Cailitin's ' Magic Clan.' Cuchullain again held them at bay till the return of the Ulster army : but it returned only in time to avenge his death, still in the prime of youth, and to complete his work.

It has been remarked that in the characters of Homer—so absolutely true are they to nature—the qualities which bear the same name are yet essentially different qualities ; as, for example, courage as illustrated in Achilles and Ajax, in Diomed and in Hector. This mark of truthfulness strikes us at once in the Tain. The kingly valour of Fergus, thoughtful and serene, has nothing in common with the animal fearlessness of Lok

Mac Favesh, or the blind patriotic fury of Ketherne, and
but little with that of Ferdia. In Cuchullain, courage is
an inspiration descending from above upon a being
essentially emotional, and though always brave, yet
sensitive and capable of awe. We smile at the boundless admiration lavished on strength by all early races ;
nor shall we understand it aright while we suppose that
it was, indeed, directed to mere physical qualities. This
was not so. Body and soul were not then thus carefully
discriminated ; the heroic deed was attributed, not to
the hand alone, but to the warrior himself, his heart
and his brain ; and not to the man only, but to some
divine aid, his because deserved by him. Cuchullain
is the chief example of heroism thus conceived. He is
slender as a maid ; but in the crisis of battle, when his
spirit kindles, his stature becomes gigantic. This
close connection between the material and the spiritual
explains the rapidity with which the wounds of these
legendary heroes heal. Should there ever come a time
when the spiritual is the chief object of man's reverence,
the present adulation of mere intellect will be looked on
as we regard the enthusiasm bestowed on martial might
in days gone by.

The imaginative literature of early races wears a
rough exterior ; but as we are told of a 'latent heat,' so

there exists a latent thoughtfulness ; and it is often
found unexpectedly in the depths of a tale which on its
surface reveals no disposition to deal with hard problems.
The reader of the Tain will be reminded of this truth
in proportion as he understands the relative position
of the Irish kingdoms at the time it describes. Connaught was the most barbaric as well as the poorest
of them all ; while Ulster had even then reached that
superiority in strength and wealth, and in civilisation
both civil and military, which for so many centuries she
retained. Her king was the subtlest and most powerful
of the Irish kings ; and her celebrated 'Red Branch
Knights' were the most gallant order of Irish chivalry.
The more astonishing, consequently, was the utter pros-
tration, a defeat without a battle, into which she so
suddenly fell. Without any apparent cause her strength
changed to weakness, and her wisdom to folly. It
was the rebuke of her pride. At the critical moment of
her fortunes her great ones began to babble and talk
nonsense. All that their country had been they forgot ;
and the near future they looked on through what the
Tain calls 'a mist of imbecility,' and attributes to witch-
craft. Equally striking is the change which takes place
when the spell is reversed. The inferior nation can
neither use nor retain the advantages accidentally and

dishonestly gained, and defeat succeeds to triumph. I know of nothing else in poetry which resembles this. Possibly it might be easier to find a parallel in history.

The Tain, a work which, while abounding in passion, distinctly includes an element of humour and irony, suffers nothing from a revulsion so strange. It ends with a great event, a battle and an overthrow; and if that catastrophe is but a 'conclusion inconclusive,' and no results remain behind, in this very circumstance lies a special significance of the work. To this issue the whole leads up, and the reader is not taken by surprise. Throughout the tale he finds the same strange mixture of ardent affections with causeless hatreds; of quick sympathies with injustice and ferocity; of high daring with a blundering the consequence not of incapacity, but of tortuous acuteness. Everywhere he finds the contrast between the emotional in excess and an all but complete absence of discipline, whether moral or mental. Such characteristics may last for centuries, but the end is ever the same—exertions that amaze, and abortive results. The only cause for surprise is that a moral so grave should have been unconsciously bequeathed by an ancient work, written to amuse, not instruct. The explanation is that a poem true to the time and to the characters it commemorates, teaches by necessity what they teach.

The relation in which St. Kiaran stood to the Tain illustrates that of the Christian priesthood to the imaginative traditions of Ireland. The living bards and the clergy could not but be rivals, but it was often a friendly rivalship ; and as regards the bards of past centuries, there was no room for jealousy. By degrees the clergy took an interest in the ancient tales, and became attached to what they befriended. Amid many extravagances they detected doubtless a significance which escapes the half-closed eye of a cynic shrewdness. Occasionally they added to old legends an interpolation which might have surprised those who had first sung them. Thus we read that Cuchullain, when going forth to his last battle, heard a choir of angels singing above that hill on which the cathedral of Armagh was destined one day to stand ; that he was pleased by the anthem, and that his pleasure in it was accepted as a homage of good-will. Elsewhere he is represented as fleeting in his war-car, after death, above his beloved Emania. He sings,—

> I played on breaths
> Above the horses' steam :
> There used to be broken before me
> Great battles on every side :

yet he ends with a warning to the race of man, and announces the day of judgment.

The teachers of those days doubtless believed that religion could afford to be indulgent towards minstrels who had been true to such lesser lights as they possessed. Paganism in those days was too little insidious to be dangerous. There is a paganism in literature much more formidable than theirs; but it had not then manifested itself. It belongs to that corrupted civilisation which uses against Christianity those intellectual and imaginative gifts, as well as that social and scientific progress, which it owes to Christianity alone. It belongs also to that merely conventional civilisation which has scanty dealings either with nature or with the supernatural. Nature, even in periods branded as 'barbaric,' has qualities that indicate a sympathy with the divine; for it has ardent affections, a simple refinement, singleness of aim, a marvellous self-sacrifice, and those unblunted sensibilities, both of love and reverence, without which the loftiest revealed truths cease to have a meaning. The heroic at its highest stretches forth its hands to the spiritual; and its very deficiencies are a confession that it needs to be supplemented by a something higher than itself. We must not confound the 'savage' state which has fallen beneath the dominion of blind sense, with the 'barbaric' which has not yet ascended into the clearer day, but which in its twilight has a gleam of coming morn. If Ireland, once converted to the faith, filled the world with her missions, there must have existed in her previously a thoughtfulness as well as a fearlessness each of which found its way at last into the nobler fields of enterprise. It is not unlikely that the apostle from Clonmacnoise and Iona often cheered his way over the Northumbrian moors or through the Teuton forest with a ballad about Cuchullain as well as with a Latin hymn of Sedulius.

The mode in which the pagan legend sometimes put on a Christian interpretation is especially illustrated in the 'Children of Lir.' Even in its later form that tale is said to be anterior to the year 1000 ; but as an oral tradition it probably existed, like the social and political conditions it records, centuries before the Christian Era. A narrative, at first but the record of some dreadful crime in a heathen household, changed by degrees into a mystic hymn on the sanctity of child-hood, its capacity for the heavenly hope, its obedience, endurance, and fidelity, its power through entire simplicity to find, in the strangest affliction, purification only and a whiter innocence. Under the trials of nine centuries those sufferers alone retain a perpetual childhood ; their father's house, and the still lake before it, stand ever before their imagination ; and the burden of the years but falls on them for a moment, to be flung aside for ever. Their 'songs in the night season,' the swan-song of a long dying, wafted over unstable waters for the solace of the strong ones dwelling on the land, imply that the martial bards of old knew in part the higher and serener function of poetry. It is significant that while the sentenced belong to the earlier Tuatha de Dannan race, the witch, while imprecating upon them the curse, addresses them thus :—' Ye of the white faces, of the stammering *Gael.*' Apparently some bard of a later day resolved that these children of an unblessed stock should be a prophetic anticipation of the Gael whose boast was his faith. There was to be again a Ruth out of Moab, one not gleaning amid the fields of promise, but scattering their earliest seed ; a Gentile with a faith not found in Israel, yet an Israelite indeed. A prose translation of this tale, among the earliest at once and the most signally modified of the Irish legends, was made by my early friend, Gerald Griffin,[1] a man who, when certain to attain the first place among Irish popular writers, passed it by for a humble one among the 'Christian Brothers.'

The 'Children of Lir' is perhaps the chief memorial of that Tuatha de Dannan race, which had held sway for two centuries before the invasion of the Gael, and yet were

---

[1] Author of *The Collegians.*

themselves regarded as intruders by the Firbolgs. Lir
and Bove, Tuathan kings, were separated by seven
centuries from 'Conn of the Hundred Fights.' The
great names of Tyr-Owen and Tyr-Conel had not risen ;
and 1,800 years had to pass before the foundations were
laid of those abbeys and castles now in ruins. Yet then,
too, there were monuments. The Tuathan might have
pointed out to his Gaelic conqueror a cairn which still
remains on the coast of Sligo, that of Eochy, King of the
Firbolgs. On the banks of the Boyne he might have
made boast of a huge sepulchral mound still shown to
the traveller, the tomb of Lewy, in whose veins the blood
of the Tuatha was blended with that of the earlier
Fomorian pirates. We know not whether the Dun-
Aengus had yet lifted its ponderous masses on Aran
Island ; but two centuries were to go by before Queen
Macha traced the foundations of Emania, and five before
Queen Meave built the palace of Cruachan. It is remarkable that while numerous Firbolg monuments, and
in some places the race itself, survive, the mediæval
genealogies include no descent from the Tuatha de
Dannan. They are described as an unwarlike race that
worked in mines, and practised magical arts—arts
through which, when dispossessed by a stronger foe,

they had 'retired into invisibility,' living an immortal life among hills and under lakes.

The 'Children of Lir,' and the 'Sons of Usnach'[1] are two of those tales which in Ireland were always known as 'the Three Sorrows of Song.' Critics who regard the 'Tain bo Cuailgné' but as a single fragment of a great Irish epic, include the second among the remaining fragments. To me it seems that each work is structurally complete in itself; but that, in spirit, the two are strikingly unlike, the 'Tain' being essentially epic, while the 'Sons of Usnach' is a tragedy cast in a narrative form. The idea of fate enters into it as strongly as into any Greek play, its heroine, the 'Babe of Destiny,' being, of all those who have a part in the tale, the one least subdued by that destiny which she strives in vain to avert. Those who charge the Irish race with a fatalism supposed to be a mark of its Eastern origin, may point to this tale as a proof that the characteristic is at least an ancient one.

It is natural to compare the Irish legends with those of other races. An eminent Irish scholar asserts that the 'Tain bo Cuailgné is to Irish history what the Argonautic expedition, and the Seven against Thebes,

[1] More correctly written Uisnach. See *Loch Etive and the Sons of Uisnach*, Macmillan & Co.

are to the Grecian.' Landor's 'Hellenics' represent many of the least known Greek legends, and his 'Gebir' might be taken for a recovered Greek 'lesser epic ;' but with such poems the Irish legends can boast little affinity. The best of the Roman have perished, except those which Livy preserved by appropriating, and which, notwithstanding their large element of fiction, constitute perhaps the most true, because the most characteristic portion of the earlier Roman history. Between the Irish and such Scandinavian legends as the celebrated 'Story of the Volsungs and Niblings' there is one striking resemblance. In each case the earliest existing prose version obviously represents a metrical work earlier still, large fragments of which survive, cropping up in it like sea rocks that indicate the hills submerged. In the 'Tain' many passages, besides those which can be called poetical, thus hold their own, apparently but because the trouble of altering them was thus evaded. That Scandinavian tale has a keen-edged, concentrated might about it, together with, at least in Mr. Morris's translation, a corresponding force and an exquisite beauty of style ; and in these respects I think it superior to the 'Tain :' but the latter will probably be deemed by impartial readers to have the advantage in imagination, varied conception of character, and pathos.

As regards comparative antiquity the 'Tain' must have preceded the Northern work by at least six centuries. The latter includes a chapter, the fourteenth, entitled 'The Welding together of the Shards of the Sword Grana,' taken, as might seem, from 'The Knighting of Cuchullain,' so close is the resemblance—as close as that between the Spanish story of the 'Monk and the Bird,' known to the English reader through Archbishop Trench's charming poem, and the Irish tale regarded as its original. The best characteristics of Irish legends, a certain swiftness and daring, a wildness of invention, a power that in its fiercest moods is often subtly combined with grace, and a tenderness as often alternated with humour, are found chiefly in the earlier. The highest inspiration of the Bards seems to have passed away not long after Ireland became Christian. 'Great Pan was dead,'—slain by the shaft of a mightier light. The further back we go the higher is the imagination, the energy, and even the art ; the legends of the Heroic Age surpassing the mediæval in refinement as much as in force, and the mediæval escaping the extravagancies and vulgarities sometimes found in those of later days. In ancient Ireland history and poetry had but a single Muse, and the bard who professed to be 'a maker' would have found no listener. Through all its changes the traditional legend claimed a foundation of truth, and pointed ever to some unmeasured antiquity. In that early springtide the hard and rugged March buds of Song were scarcely distinguishable from the rough rind of fact out of which they had pushed.

The present work concludes a series of poems intended to illustrate Irish history at its chief periods. The 'Legends of St. Patrick' deal with Ireland's 'saintly time,' and 'Inisfail' with those six centuries between the Norman invasion and the repeal of the penal laws in the latter half of the eighteenth century—a period calamitously misrepresented by partisan historians ; one in which the wild passions and wilder political theories which, since the first French Revolution, have in so many countries directed high aspirations to mean or fatal ends, had no existence ; a period of which 'all the struggles were characterised by the spirit of liberty, nor less by that of loyalty, whether directed to Gaelic princes, to Norman chiefs who had become Irish, to Charles, or James.'[1] Another period remained, that of Ireland's 'Heroic Age.' This volume is a contribution to its illustration. I trust that the poets of a later day will illustrate it more worthily, and do for Irish history what the lofty and stainless poetry of Scott did for that of his country.

[1] Advertisement to 'Inisfail,' p. 52.

The theme is large ; and the quarry, so rich in materials, is as yet scarcely opened. Notwithstanding the destruction of numberless Irish books which certainly existed as late as 1631, and the yet larger number known to have been extant in the eleventh century, besides the vast collections which perished during the Danish invasions, we are informed that the Irish books still preserved in Trinity College, Dublin, and the Royal Irish Academy would alone fill 30,000 quarto pages. These volumes exist, almost all of them, in MS. only ; while a few, which, without State aid or any public encouragement, have been translated, remain unprinted—a circumstance not honourable either to Ireland's patriotism, or to that love of learning once her boast. A mere fragment of the remaining surplus from the Irish Church property would restore to light all the best specimens of ancient Irish genius for the benefit not of Ireland's sons only, but of learning in all lands ; and she has still scholars competent to the task. Those who cannot study the originals may wish to know where they may find some valuable translations. Several have appeared in the 'Atlantis,' a periodical established in connection with the Catholic University of Ireland when Cardinal Newman was its rector, in the publications of the 'Ossianic Society,' of the 'Irish Archæological and Celtic

Society,' and of the 'Kilkenny Archæological Society.'
The English reader is more likely to be already acquainted
with Dr. O'Donovan's great translation of the 'Annals of
the Four Masters;' with the works of Dr. Petrie, of Dr.
Todd, and Dr. Reeves; with the 'Tripartite Life of St.
Patrick,' translated, as well as many ancient tales, by
Mr. W. M. Hessessy; with Dr. Joyce's 'Old Celtic
Romances;' and with Mr. Standish O'Grady's brilliant
bardic 'History of Ireland.' How entirely early Irish
legends are susceptible of a high poetic rendering in our
own day can be doubted by no one who has read the
poems founded on them which we owe to the genius of
Sir Samuel Ferguson.[1]

[1] 1. Lays of the Western Gael. 2. Congal. 3. Poems. By
Sir Samuel Ferguson. Bell and Sons.

CONTENTS.

THE SONS OF USNACH

TO THE MEMORY

OF

EUGENE O'CURRY,

FIRST PROFESSOR OF IRISH HISTORY IN THE
CATHOLIC UNIVERSITY OF IRELAND,

THIS POEM

IS DEDICATED.

THE SONS OF USNACH.

CANTO THE FIRST.

In Felim's house they kept the royal feast.
  And all the echoing hall with tumult rang.
Tumult that still from morn to eve increased ;
  And now the tale they told, and now they sang.
Chief minstrel he to Conor, Uladh's [1] lord,
Who graced that day, as oft, his favourite's board.

Sudden to Felim's seat a woman rushed,
  An ancient nurse with wrinkled face and worn
Clamouring, her hands upheld and forehead flushed,
  ' Felim, rejoice ! for lo, thy babe is born !
And proud be thou, for goodlier is this child
Than e'er till now on proudest parent smiled !

[1] Ulster.

These tidings heard, yet higher swelled the acclaim ;
　　The Red Branch Knights oft pledged that infant's
　　　　health,
And prayed that all high gifts of wealth and fame,
　　Great lordship, and great valour, and great wealth
Might grace its life, and in the far-off days
Compass its head with everlasting praise.

But when an hour had passed, and somewhat more,
　　The feasters heard far off a dulcet strain,
And soon to them there entered damsels four ;
　　With measured step advanced they twain by twain,
Bearing a cradle.　On a low-raised throne
They reared it, bowered in silk, and blossom-strewn.

Therein a little maiden-wonder lay
　　Unlike all babes besides in mien and hue,
Bright as a lily-bud at break of day
　　That flashes through the night's unlifted dew :
Beaming her eyes ; like planets glad and fair :
And o'er her forehead curved a fringe of hair.

The tender fairy hand, whose substance fine
　　Glimmered as of compacted moonbeams made
With such a stealthy smoothness did it shine,
　　Above the coverlet unquiet strayed ;
And some one said, ' It knows the things to be,
And seeks its wand of destined empery ! '

From bannered stalls the Red Branch Knights drew nigh
  Circling that cradle.   'Neath the raftered roof
A far-sunk window opened to the sky,
  While purple twilight wove with warp and woof
O'er deepening heavens its dewy mantle dark,
And dusking woods, that hour unseen ; when, hark

Outside that casement rang a piercing wail ;
  Then, past it slow, a dread and shrouded Form
On demon wings was seen of all to sail :
  Shriek after shriek out-swelled into a storm :
And o'er that flower new-born of infancy
All heard the Banshee's death-denouncing cry.

Then, from his seat in that high hall remote
  Whereon all day in silence he had sate
Advanced, unguided, to that Infant's cot
  Cathbad, the Druid old, and man of Fate,
And o'er that infant held his arms out-spread,
And raised to heaven his grey and sightless head

At last he spake, 'This day a woe to man,
  And yet the crown of woman's kind, is born :
This day is sent a blessing and a ban ;
  She shall be black as night, and white as morn ;
And lo, upon her cheek I see such red
As stains great warriors on the war-field dead.

'A death to mighty hosts that face shall be :
  Through her a king shall pass to banishment :
Through her shall perish Usnach's peerless Three ;
  Through her from sacred Eman's [1] roofs fire-rent
Even now I see the reddening smoke-cloud leap :
Deirdré her name.   Through her shall widows weep.'

King Conor heard, and in his angry mood
  Had risen to speak her doom ; 'That child shall die !'
Save that the Uladh nobles where they stood
  The king forestalling, hurled abroad their cry ;
'She must not live !'   Of all those knights but two
Will'd not that deed—the bravest Erin knew.

For at that hour upon the cradle's right
  Stood Conal Carnach ; at its left, though young,
Swifter in chase, and stronger yet in fight,
  Cuchullain.   Neither swelled that shout of wrong.
Once more it rose : but Conor ne'er was known
To walk in any counsel save his own.

He spake : 'She shall not die : this babe I take,
  My ward, until her destinies be known :
An isle tower-girt is mine in yonder lake :
  There shall she live ; and there shall live alone :

[1] Eman, also called Emania, stood nearly on the present site of Armagh.

By none that fatal beauty shall be seen :
Full-grown the maid perchance may be my queen.'

Wondering they heard, but no man made reply,
   For Conor's will was lord to all and each,
A man of counsel deep, and purpose high,
   In action sudden, sparing of his speech :
Early he won the people to his will :
Ere long they feared him : but they loved him still.

While yet a child, the stepson of that king
   Who reigned in Uladh, Fergus son of Roy,
Conor had shared his home.   That prince would bring
   Oft to his judgment court Queen Nessa's boy
Whose forward wit unravelled every suit,
Delighting in the wrangling clan's dispute.

Fergus was loftier-minded : ever more
   He loathed the sordid plea, the varnished wrong.
And inly scorned the Ollamh's learnèd lore :
   More dear to him the chase, the feast, the song :
Wearied one day, he cried with laughing face,
' Conor ! speak thou the judgment in my place ! '

The boy made answer none ; but instant bowed,
   And judgment gave so full, so just, so clear,
A shout rang upward from the astonished crowd,
   ' Worthy of kingship thou ! ' His crowned compeer.

Fergus arose ; incensed he made reply ;
' Throne him your king, if worthier he than I ! '

Conor since then had ruled the Ulidian race,
    And ever waxed in subtlety and power,
Though better loved was Fergus' honest face,
    And princely port, forth issuing from his tower
At times with horse and hound to chase the boar,
Crowning at times the topmost ridge of war.

Conor was loved and feared : one clan alone
    Nor feared, nor loved him, Usnach's : and the king
In Usnach's house a rival to his throne
    Or noting, or belike imagining,
Still watched that house to crush it, had he dared ;
But Uladh loved it, and her monarch spared.

Meantime to that green island in the lake
    The years came softly : softly went they by
As like as snowy flake to snowy flake,
    As like as smile to smile, as sigh to sigh ;
And as some flower that feeds on beams and dew
Its inmate rose in beauty ever new,

Deirdré. With her abode an ancient dame,
    The tale-recounter of the royal court
In years departed ; Levarcam her name :
    None other to that island made resort

Save now and then treading the downward rocks
Some shepherd with the firstling of his flocks.

Beauteous as heaven that gladsome captive was ;
   With every month more fair, more gladsome grew ;
Her pastime, counting jewels in the grass,
   Emerald and amethyst, and sapphire blue,
Or chasing—never part had she in sloth—
From bloom to bloom the evening-gilded moth.

Impassioned friendships hers with every kind :
   To her the Robin came ; to her the Hare ;
And still with insight flashed from heart to mind,
   She guessed their lives in tree or bosky lair,
Sharing their vernal joys, and, when the snows
Besieged their haunts, condoling with their woes.

Inquisitive the creature was, and brave :
   From rock to rock alone she roamed ; untaught
She knew to climb the tree and swim the wave ;
   Soaring and swift, for knowledge still she sought,
Nor sought in vain, far wiser than she wist ;
Infantine minstrel, and mythologist.

For when she heard the wintry tempests raving,
   Fables she told of immemorial feuds,
And warring Gods that still, for vengeance craving,
   Devastated some rival's peaceful woods ;

And when the morning shone, serene and mild,
She laughed and said, 'These Gods are reconciled !'

Betwixt that island and the forest green
   A causeway stretched.   Scorning King Conor's law,
O'er it in summer maidens tripped unseen,
   And told her tales of all they heard and saw,
And flowers in May, and fruits in summer brought her,
Or with her danced beside the moonlit water.

Two men alone she saw ; at times the king :
   His grizzled beard and searching eye she fled,
And wept to think that in some far-off spring
   She must be his.   That thought alone with dread
Touched her keen instinct.   In that face august
Something unblest she saw, and ill to trust.

Yet oft he came, watching that flower of beauty
   That still from crude, reluctant bud emerged ;
And citing still past vow, and future duty
   Impledged thereby ; and still with presents urged ;
And ever reaped for such more scoffs than gain—
Officious is his zeal whose hope is vain !

The other visitor she better loved,
   A Druid, silver-headed : to her isle
Daily he came, a teacher well-approved ;
   And much he taught her, with his grave calm smile

Advancing still into his pupil's heart :
To elicit thence, he knew, was to impart.

He taught her all a monarch's bride had need
   In those old days to learn.   Devout and grave,
He taught her all the Ogham signs to read,
   Inscribed on mossy stone or mystic stave ;
And how to trace green Erin's Kings, each one
To Heber or Heremon, Ir, or Donn.

One morn as on their glories he descanted,
   ' Where are they now ? ' his wondering listener said ;
Then silent stood, like shape to stone enchanted :
   But when he answered sadly, ' They are dead,'
She bounded t'ward the on-wavering butterfly,
And cried, ' At least he lives ; and so do I ! '

Once too she caught that Druid by the sleeve,
   And spake ; ' Great Master, this I ask of thee !
Who was it made the sun, the morn and eve,
   The stars, the flying clouds, the boundless sea ? '
Her great wide eyes, clasped hands, and lips com-
      pressed,
Better than words enforced the unending quest.

The Druid answered, dubious, still refining
   With stress and strain of profluent words that left
The problem's jet-black surface smooth and shining
   But ne'er the mystery's heart of marble cleft,

And ended ; 'God is God :—but ah, the woe !
That which God is, not even the Druids know ! '

' Then God must be a God who hides Himself
    In sport, or else for cause we know not of !
And doubtless,' thus ran on the careless elf,
    ' Who hides in sport will show His face in love ;
Much seeking will not find Him.   He will come
Then when He wills ; and take His children home.

' For I remember once in yonder wood
    My nurse, to mock me, hid her in an oak,
Whilst idly I a dragon-fly pursued :
    I missed her soon : I wept : then forth she broke !
Thus likewise God, hearing His creatures moan,
Will flash on them, and cry, "Mine own, mine own ! "

' That day the wise will serve Him ; but the fool
    Will sport with Ogham stave, or dragon-fly
That lights his spark—lo there—on dusky pool !
    Of those that sport at once, and serve am I !
Therefore, come quickly, God !   And thou, good stave,
Fly hence ! '   And forth she flung it on the wave !

But when she found within the Master's face,
    Not wrath—for that she looked—but awe-struck woe,
A change there passed, too swift for eye to trace,
    Athwart her rain-dark eyes, and front of snow ;

And straight the child, by love's remorse possessed,
Kissed with her whole bright face that Druid's breast.

The years passed by ; and, onward as they sped,
   That child from beauty still to beauty grew ;
In her, full many a fair one came and fled
   Like sunny gleams that each the last pursue ;
And yet that glad succession brought no change ;
Each child in turn was wilful, sweet, and strange.

Older, beyond her island bounds she strayed
   Despite the king ; for, ever since her birth,
Of nought that tender heart had been afraid :
   Banshee, or ghost, she heard of, now with mirth,
And now with awe, but never with affright ;
And gladly would have faced them if she might.

Not so old Levarcam ! a spasm of dread
   ' Oft blanched her cheek remembering Conor's word,
' Keep safe the child, or forfeit is thy head ! '
   In Deirdré's absence, if a leaf but stirred
She shook ; and endless tales, and legends told
To keep her young lamb safe within the fold.

She told how first, from regions of the morn
   With black-sailed ships stemming the ocean tide
To Erin's forest, yet of men forlorn,
   Came Partholan, the Grecian Parricide :

And how the ill race had perished.   Deirdré cried
With reddening cheek ; 'Glad am I that they died ! '

Then, with a brightening in her old, pale face,
 Her nurse resumed : 'But we—the Gael—but we,
The offspring are we of a lordlier race,
 The heirs of some diviner destiny !
King Miledh was our sire !   From far Espán
His dauntless sons led forth the Gaedil clan.'

Of Scota next she told, the widowed Queen ;
 And how that sad one left her lonely throne
Girt by eight sons ; and how, with eye serene,
 She marked above the wine-black ocean prone
The monsters rise ; nor feared to watch the wave
Heaven-high, anon descending to its grave.

Time on her brow had graved no characters ;
 Sorrow no splendour stol'n from that wide eye
That ever, as the legend old avers,
 Reposed on some far seat of sovereignty
By others hoped ;—to her alone revealed
Beyond sea-cloud, and ocean's heaving field.

She saw the waves engulf the drowning decks ;
 Yet nought could scare that eye, or blanch that cheek :
Four sons she saw upon their mastless wrecks
 High driven on Erin's rocks and headlands bleak

From Inver Scena to the house of Donn :
She said ; 'The price is paid ; the Isle is won ! '

She saw the victory's prelude and no more ;
   Half-way 'twixt ocean marge and mountain crest
Where sleep the Great Ones of the days of yore
   Early she made her venerable rest,
And holds, well-pleased, an ever-spreading fame,
Sealing a mighty people with her name.[1]

Not all the themes were war : the fabler told
   Of Feale, the dusk-eyed beauty of the South,
By Lewy won mid olive forests old :
   Such minstrelsies went freshening from his mouth
That in his hand her own the princess placed,
Nor feared, his wife, to dare the wan sea-waste.

She told how, later, by that northern tide
   A blush of causeless shame her cheek had stained :
And how, heart-grieved at fancied wrong, she died,
   Where wrong was none ; and how her husband
      plained
Year after year, while she, at Scota's feet,
Rested revered where earth and ocean meet.

  [1] The Irish, originally ' Scoti,' were so called from Scota.

Next told she how for Tara's King they found
   No consort worthy of the royal bed
From east to west through Erin's utmost bound ;
   And how, dream-warned, the youth had northward
     sped :
And how, from fountain-bower by Fairy Brugh,
A white maid looked on him with eyes of blue.

And how that beauteous phantom, Eadane,
   Had laid a hand like light upon his hair ;
And next, lest he should die of yearnings vain,
   Assumed a woman's form, though woven of air ;
And borne him pretty babes within their bower ;
Yet ofttimes bade him 'ware the destined hour.

And how at Tara, while the nobles sate
   Gracing his feast, that queen sent forth a cry :
And how the Fairy-King through guards and gate
   Passed swiftly, mailed in dew-like jewelry,
And like a whirlwind bore in sight of all,
The Fairy Princess to her father's hall !

While thus the tales ran on, the years ran by,
   Tales, some of sadness, some of mirth and jest,
Till now the child to maiden prime was nigh :
   The tales of war and wonder pleased her best :

The love-tales well began, no doubt : yet all
Ended, she thought, in something slight and small.

And still whate'er she heard of good and pure
   Within the virgin's memory held its place
Like names on tree-stems graved that aye endure :
   Of questionable things survived no trace :
They passed, like letters written in a rill
That upward laughs to heaven, re-virgined still.

One day it chanced that, while the March wind's breath
   Was softening round the daffodil's first bud,
Their shepherd old had saved a lamb from death,
   And slain the wolf, and in their gateway stood ;
And, as the wounded creature bled, below
A crimson blood-pool stained the last night's snow.

Sudden there swooped to earth a raven black,
   And feasted on that blood.   As in a dream
The maiden watched it long : at last she spake,
   Whilst o'er her grave face ran a laughing gleam,
' These be Love's colours, black and red, and white ;—
Yet love we know, is nought, when judged aright !

' These be Love's colours, white and black, and red :—
   Some little foolish maid, to love inclined,

Might say : " Though all should love me none shall
    wed
  Until in one dear face those three I find ;
Not raven locks alone, or front of snow,
But on the heroic cheek the battle's glow !"'

Beside the girl stood Levarcam ; she smiled,
  And spake ; 'Good sooth, your shaft hath hit its mark;
Yea doubtless, you were born a prophet's child !
  For Naisi's front is white, his tresses dark ;
And still of him men say ; " On Naisi's cheek
Not roses, but red dawns of battles break !"'

Then to the flash from Deirdré's peerless eyes
  Her nurse made answer ; 'Naisi ! who is he ?
Warrior there treads not under Erin's skies
  But knows the man ! the swiftest of those Three !
No hounds they need ! alone they chase, each morn,
The stag, and downward drag him head and horn !

Ever at Uladh's feasts the clansmen say
  'Set ye the sons of Usnach side by side,
A rock behind them, or some cromlech grey,
  Then blow a trump o'er Erin, far and wide ;
And range her hosts against them, face to face,
Those Three shall hew them down, and homeward
    chase !

Their singing is the best all Uladh boasts ;
  Of all her sons most courteous they and kind ;
To heaven devoutest of her countless hosts :
  Softly along his path they lead the blind ;
Submission made, no more remember ill ;
Nor ever kissed a maid against her will.

To these the clans send embassies from far
  Laden with gifts, and suing, " Grant us aid !
Rule us in battle's hour, and head our war ! "
  But women say, " How well their mother prayed
For sons both mild and valiant ! " Lo, a ray
Of her sweet countenance lives in theirs this day ! '

Here Levarcam a moment stopped for breath ;
  Then Deirdré rose and sought the neighbouring
      strand :
Ice-bound it was, and cold that hour as death :
  To her 'twas warm as mead by May breeze fanned
She paced along its pebbly beach for hours :
And to her feet its shingles felt like flowers.

Returned, more lofty looked she than at morn :
  With more of inward gladness, yet less gay ;
More confident, though lost her girlish scorn
  In some half womanhood's benigner ray :
Smiling, she met her nurse's smile, and then
' Naisi,' she said, ' will love me ! Who cares when ? '

c

The maiden paused ; she mused ; again she spake,
  Fixing on Levarcam those marvellous eyes ;
' Three be Love's colours—white, and red, and black :
  White, for the sake of Love's white sanctities ;
And red, for Love must war on many a foe ;
And black, since Love, though crowned, must end in woe.'

Again she mused :—' Yes, Love must war ! Who fears ?
  Though Love must fight, he fights in love, not hate !
Some glorious conflict rages through the years ;
  Great Love must take therein his part, elate.
And woe comes last.   On raven pinions borne
Night comes not less :—but after night comes morn !'

From that time Naisi's name she named no more ;
  Nothing she seemed to lack ; nothing to crave :
Her heart through spiritual realms was strong to soar,
  Self-lifted as from windless seas the wave ;
A spirit of strength from earthly bonds escaped
She trod ; her body's self but spirit draped ;

A spirit of strength and swiftness onward borne
  Through luminous realms, all resonant and free,
Happier because unwinged, like endless morn
  With silver feet circling the spherèd sea :
And still her lonely thought with song was blent ;
And bird-like still she warbled as she went.

For music then, like warfare, not from art
   Grew up laborious :—born of frank good-will,
'Twas Joy's loud clarion in the generous heart ;
   Through pains more perfect grew the harper's skill :
Yet still from purest soul, and noblest breast
The minstrelsy perforce became the best.

Deirdré besides, on Naisi's music musing—
   That strain far-famed she once had heard in dream—
Through some strange craft of Nature's sweet infusing
   Unconscious copied it. A lily's gleam
Shines thus, reflected in the lake below,
More softly, green for green, and snow for snow.

Once too she marked two mated eagles flying
   Far from their cliff, her little lake above,
Sunward in strength, and clapped her hands loud crying,
   'On, wedded Spirits, on ! for this is Love !
No woodland murmurs yours, and thraldom none !
Sail on till buried in the ascending sun !'

That vision shaped her life. Through wild and wood
   Long hours that morn had Naisi chased the stag :
It took the wave and vanished. Silent stood
   At noon the hunter on a jutting crag :
His eye upon a tower-crowned island fell ;
Thereon it fastened, bound as by a spell.

'There lies,' he mused, 'that wondrous-countenanced
    child,
    Like some poor bird a captive from its birth,
In that lone island year by year exiled :
    How little she suspects her grace and worth !
Our household foe ere long will clutch that hand—
Is yon a causeway leading to the land ? '

An hour had fled, and lo ! that bridge he paced ;
    Ere long, no child, but, sparkling like a flower,
The imprisoned maid, nor startled nor shame-faced,
    Passed by the youth, advancing from her bower
With breeze-like step, yet down-dropp'd lids of snow :
'Ah foot,' he cried, ' more light than foot of doe ! '

An instant back she flashed her magic eyes
    And from her laughing lip the answer leaped,
'Where stags are none, the doe must monarchise ! '
    Some ballad old it was, but never steeped
Till then with such strange sweetness to his ear :
Was it reproof or challenge, vague yet dear ?

Naisi rejoined ; 'A monarch rules this land ;
    For you he destines Erin's proudest throne !
Ah, but for that how many a warrior's brand '—
    ' His realm,' she said, ' is his : my heart mine own :
A maiden I have lived : maiden would die : '
The warrior fixed on hers his strong grey eye.

That eye, though young and sweet with such clear light,
   Had marshalled many a death-strewn battle-field ;
Had watched the meeting tides of many a fight ;
   Taught many a proud, inviolate fort to yield.
With gaze as frank and clear thus answered she,
' I know you well ! the eldest of those Three !

' Where are your brothers ? She whom nurse I call
   Has told me all the Three are kind and brave :
Fain would I sister be to each and all :
   Fain too my life from love tyrannic save ! '
' Their sister you shall be,' the youth replied ;
' Mine if you will ; but none the less my bride ! '

He spake ; then, for the maiden's safety fearing,
   With passion changed continued ; ' Spurn my suit !
The king will slay thee ! ' She, the warrior nearing,
   Held forth both hands, and gazed upon him mute :
And last, in love's high truth—and truth is best—
Made answer ; ' Thine ! ' He snatched her to his
     breast.

Thence lifting soon a countenance glad yet tearful,
   She spake ; ' Your knighthood stands consummate
     now !
Since a true maid, of Conor's wrath not fearful,
   Has heard, and with her own has crowned your vow.

Forth, on your task decreed !   Fly hence, and prove
Ten years in battle-fields what might hath Love !

' In ten years bring me back your trophied spoils
    From every land and clime ; for mine they are !
I that inspired, can well requite your toils :
    Ever till then, my spirit like a star,
Shall o'er you hang !   Farewell ! yet, ere you go,
Sing ! for how great your songs long since I know.'

So, hand in hand, upon that causeway standing,
    Those youthful lovers measure after measure
Poured forth, their bosoms more and more expanding
    At once with music's zeal, and love's pure pleasure ;
For Deirdré still her voice with Naisi's twined,
All-perfect harmony though undesigned.

And though till then no war-song she had sung
    That hour her song grew warlike as his own !
And, o'er her heaven-like beauty as he hung,
    His war-songs tender grew, and sweet of tone :
And still they sang, till now through woods loud ringing
The men of Erin, east and west, came winging,

And found those lovers in that lonely haunt,
    That sunset round them glowing and above ;
And saw the forests flash, the blue waves pant ;
    And heard that mingled praise of war and love :—

Then ceased that pair, and softly smiled, and said,
'What makes us glad is this ; we two are wed !'

But when, to many a questioner replying,
    They found that they had only met that noon,
The lovers laughed a sweet-voiced laughter, crying,
    'We thought we had been wedded many a moon !
Great love, it seems, lives long in little time ;
Yet shall great love be ever in his prime !

'Perchance of us some future bard shall say,
    Their bright, swift life went o'er them like a breath
Of stormy southwind in the merry May ;
    And brief their unfeared, undivided death :
For unto those who love, and love aright,
Life is Love's day ; and Death his long, sweet night.'

But straight the men of Erin cried aloud,
    'The king, the king !' and Naisi's brothers twain,
Ainli and Ardan, though to help him vowed
    At need, not less to break that troth were fain :
'Beware,' they cried ; 'since Cathbad long ago
Foretold that Babe was born for Uladh's woe !'

Yet, when within those lovers' eyes they saw
    Wild mirth alone, and blank astonishment,
They deemed the thing divine ; and, though with awe,
    Their spirits on the high adventure bent,

And council took, and with one mind decreed
That self-same night o'er Uladh's bound to speed.

This therefore was the order of their going :
    A hundred warriors marching in the van ;
A hundred maidens next with veils loose flowing ;
    A hundred clansmen next of Usnach's clan,
And each a greyhound leading in a cord ;
Swiftly with these they trod the moonlit sward.

So well were Usnach's sons both loved and feared
    King Conor could but rail against the wrong :
All round the isle they marched with banner reared,
    And trumpet blown, and many a tale and song,
Welcomed in court and camp both near and far,
From Esro's[1] Falls to sea-beat Binedar.[2]

Nathless through Conor's craft such toils were woven
    'Twixt them and Erin's Kings, to spare that wrong
Felt at low hearths when royal pacts are cloven,
    They built by northern Moyle a fleet ere long,
And spread their sails from Kermnah Dûn, and o'er
The grey-green billows sailed to Alba's shore.

      [1] Ballyshannon.   [2] Howth.

CANTO THE SECOND.

O NOBLE Alba, Scotia later named,
    Then when the race of Scota and her Lord
O'er all thy holy isles and highlands famed
    Had raised the Gaelic harp, the Gaelic sword,
And Kenneth, Pictish rule extinguished, reared
That throne of kings for centuries revered !

Great land of Alba ! in that hour supreme
    Conqueror, not conquered, wert thou ! Thy great
        heart,
Flinging from off it, like a nightmare dream,
    A sway ignobler, chose the better part,
Throning the lofty spirit in lofty place :
It brought thee bliss and bale, but nothing base !

When, centuries earlier, stood on Alba's coast
    Usnach's brave sons, her king received them well :
Treaty they made : they joined to his their host,
    And taught him soon the insurgent tribes to quell,

Yet still they loved him not : ' His soul is mean,'
They said ; 'by him shall Deirdré ne'er be seen.'

Yet near his court they dwelt ; and once it chanced
   A palace churl while o'er the forest boughs
New leaved, the earliest beam of morning glanced,
   Made way, with missives sent, to Naisi's house,
And on by dusky doors, though timorous, crept,
And found at last that room where Naisi slept.

Before its stony threshold slumbering lay
   Ainli and Ardan, clasping, each, a sword,
For ever wont were these by night and day
   Their brother and their sister thus to ward :
The intruder o'er them stepp'd and entrance made
To where in sleep that princely pair were laid.

Between them stretched from pillow on to pillow
   The massive trail of Deirdré's luminous hair,
Like gold-touched tendrils of a budded willow
   Breeze-blown against the dawn.   Already there
The greedy, youngling sunrise made his feast,
Though still in cloud half muffled was the east.

Longer that churl had stood save that in sleep
   Growled the great wolf-hound couched beside the bed :
The traitor turned ; and, skilled to crawl and creep,
   Reached the half open gates, and homeward fled,

And found the king new-risen, and nodding spake,
' Rejoice, great monarch, for thy kingdom's sake !

' Till now thou hast not found a woman meet
   In all thy land the royal throne to share ;
Behold, the loveliest lady and most sweet
   Of all the earth is near, and thou not 'ware !
Compared with her the rest are sheep and kine—
Bid Naisi die ! his consort crown as thine !'

Then told the man his tale from first to last
   With added circumstance. The Pict replied
Well pleased, albeit at Naisi's name aghast,
   ' To slay that chief were hard ; to snare his bride
Were sweet. In secret traffic with her ! Say,
She must be first my love ; my queen one day !'

Forth sped the accursed one on his mission foul,
   And came on Deirdré singing all alone,
And took his stand, ill visaged as a Ghoul,
   And named the terms, base love and future throne :
And she with darkening eyes no word replied
Save this alone ; ' Till I return, abide !'

Swiftly she walked : she came where stood the Three ;
   Then from her white lips rushed her wrong like flame ;
' Dishonoured wife !' she cried, ' with me, with me,
   Though not the treason, lives for aye the shame !

Ah, surely never wife such scorn has known
Unless the fault was first in part her own !'

But Naisi smiled, forth issuing with his brand,
　　And said but this ; 'Abide till I return ;'
And soon, that head ill-omened in his hand,
　　Came back with countenance bright, at once and
　　　　stern :
Then　Deirdré　spake,　'My　hand　had　borne　that
　　freight
If thine had spared it !　At the bad king's gate

Lay first that head, and march we hence this night !'
　　The Brothers answered ; 'No ! nor yet three days !'
Three days in pride they paced a neighbouring height:
　　Three days the Pict, thus challenged, stood at gaze,
And ofttimes grimly turned from lord to lord :
They answered nought ; nor any raised his sword.

But when the fourth dawn o'er the forest soaring
　　Sent through the heavens divergent beams of
　　　　splendour,
Upon the earth glory and gladness pouring,
　　That host arose ; nor took they farewell tender :
Three stones the clansman, each, above his head
Flung backward far in scorn : then forth they sped.

And, lest the sun should dazzle Deirdré's eyes,
   Westward that morn their pilgrimage began :
First, under standards bright with myriad dyes,
   A hundred Usnach warriors led the van :
Maids next : then clansmen, holding, each, a hound
That strained against the leash with bark and bound.

Ere long their march was through the misty highlands :
   They tracked Glenorchy's immemorial woods ;
Loch Lomond's bosky mountain-skirts and islands ;
   Birch-braided Katrine's sylvan solitudes ;
And where on shores of Fyne, now low now higher,
With punctual tide the salt sea floods respire.

Meantime the natives of those lonely regions
   Came fiercely forth from many a distant shore
Though worsted oft, in ever thickening legions,
   Till now the foray swelled into the war ;
And still there flocked from Uladh's coast in swarms
Her noblest youth, their great one's mates in arms.

For still, beside the spring her pitcher watching,
   The maid would sing of Naisi's strength and fleetness,
Ofttimes in turn on breeze of evening catching
   Some shepherd's song of Deirdré's truth and sweetness:
And still they ended, each ; ' Ill deed, King Conor,
That banished such ! Alas, the land's dishonour ! '

With varying fortune long time raged the feud :
    Clan Usnach triumphed now : anon the foe :
And oft, a swordless warrior mild of mood,
    Amid those Three was Deirdré seen : and lo !
Still, as the radiance bickers round the gem,
So flashed the battle's flame round her and them.

Thus lived they prosperous mid that storm of war,
    In victory glad, not downcast in defeat :
Three winter months when fortune pressed them sore
    Within a western isle they made retreat,
The nearest of those rock-bound Hebrides
Set mid the crystal splendour of the seas.

With Spring-tide back returned they.   Victory's sun
    Full-orbed that April on their banners played :
A third part of the realm their valour won :
    Last, with the Picts alliance firm they made,
And making kept.   All things thenceforth went well ;
And gladsome were their sports on field and fell.

It was that season when the spirit of joy
    Runs million-footed forth through earth and air :
When the hale shepherd grows once more the boy ;
    The girl-like youth is prompt to do and dare ;
When womanhood looks softer than its wont ;
The star shines whiter on the infant's front.

It was that season when the maiden's heart,
  Though guarded, faster beats against its bound;
When Love's long hidden fount, by happier art
  Divined, is nearer to the surface found :
When to the faded cheek returns its bloom ;
And tears less bitter stain the flower-decked tomb.

It was that season when on fields late dreary
  Thickest at dawn the awakened daisy throngeth ;
When in the dim sweet gloaming, never weary,
  Latest her song the darkling thrush prolongeth ;
And pillow-spurning children fret for morn,
Fresh flowers, new leaves, and ecstacies re-born.

Ah then to Naisi, and to Deirdré then
  Like fire the gladness of the spring-tide came :
That causeway old they seemed to tread again,
  Sang the same song ! Love's wild, yet vestal flame
Caught them once more as on that first of May ;
And three glad wedded years became a day.

Then, dawn by dawn, ere yet the low-tongued wind
  From unreluctant buds their sweets was wooing,
While earliest shafts through ragged fissures blind
  Of cloud forth flashed, the flying night pursuing,
Those brothers and that sister clomb the crag
And blew the horn, and roused the antlered stag.

O joy his course through woodland gulfs to follow,
　Deirdré and they, to Etive's salt sea lake !
To hear from shadowy cliff and cavern hollow
　Through glistening air the clarion's echo break,
And mark, o'er wide green plain, and purple mere,
The mountain-wall its glooming bastion rear

More high when seen through mist : to watch it
　　quivering ;
　From rock to cloud to track the eagle's flight ;
And then, close by, on spray shining and shivering,
　To mark the tender-footed bird alight,
Or flower down-bending 'neath the silenced bee,
Or gleam from rill remote on-winding noiselessly !

And O, to hear in woods the loud hounds baying,
　Or plunge of floods adown some hoarse ravine !
Or watch, from far, the waves o'er sea-ledge swaying :
　Thence refluent dragged in trails of grassy green :
Or, farther yet, that surge forever hoary
Seething round lone tormented promontory !

Three tents they planted where the forest's skirt
　Sheltered the lowland from the increasing heat ;
In one, with hand assiduous and expert,
　Deirdré prepared that food by toil made sweet ;
In one they held their banquet ; and in one
Sang their glad songs till half the night was done.

And many a night on Etive's flowery margin
  She moved, while moonbeams glazed the purple wave,
Happiest of wives ; light-footed as a virgin ;
  Or at the entrance of some ivied cave
Sang note prolonged that ended oft in laughter—
Sweet were the days, pledging some sweet hereafter !

One night, when Naisi to his rest had passed,
  Deirdré, long lingering at the bridal door,
Her eyes on Ainli and on Ardan cast,
  Great eyes with tears unused all misted o'er,
And took their hands, and spake, in low, soft tone,
'To you my Naisi's weal is as your own !

'But you, like Naisi, must have, each, your bride,
  Unhumbled maids not willing to be wed,
To walk in glorying gladness at your side :
  Find such, and I round each a silver thread
Will twine ; and bring the creatures to you bound :
Discrowned the proud must be ; and Love be crowned!"

The heroic song hath sorrows, but not sighs :
  The heroic legend tender is, yet hard ;
With grief alike, and joy, can sympathise,
  Yet keeps the heroic heart from weakness barred.
Love's 'stormy southwind' three glad years had blown:
Then Fate, that rules the nations, claimed her own.

D

Thus it befell ; once more at Conor's call
   The Red-Branch Knights partook their monarch's
     feast,
Ranged 'neath their standards round Emania's hall :
   And when at last the hunger rage had ceased,
And many an echo of loud songs had died,
King Conor rose, thus speaking in his pride ;

'What say ye, Lords ?   Deem ye that kinglier cheer,
   Or palace more majestic under sun,
Gladdens mankind than those that greet us here ?'
   They answered, 'Feast or house like thine is none ! '
Through the great hall the acclaim unmeasured brake :
It sank ; and once again King Conor spake ;

' How say ye, Lords, for leave ye have to speak ;
   That which ye think, reveal : all doubts repel ;
Find ye in Uladh aught decayed or weak,
   Amiss, or lacking ?   Or are all things well ?'
And they made answer ; 'All things right we find,
Nor aught deficient.   King, we speak our mind ! '

Yet once again, King Conor rose and said,
   ' My mind is other-minded, Lords, than yours ;
For I, though ne'er by random counsel swayed,
   Far less by murmurs low of kernes and boors,
Find this amiss—that Usnach's sons this day
For one bad woman's sake are far away ;

'A loss to Uladh, and to me the most,
  Lacking our bravest.'   Then the vast acclaim
Burst louder thrice from that exulting host ;
  And thus they cried ; 'We feared the royal blame,
And therefore hid our counsel ; but that morn
Those Three return, old Uladh stands re-born.'

Again the plot-deviser rose and spake :
  'Men of great stomachs, Lords, we count those
      Three :
" Exiles," they sware, "we go : but ne'er come back
  Till sureties strong are ours, and guarantee
By Conor sent, firm pledge of endless troth :"
Thus Naisi sware : and sacred is an oath.

'Likewise thus vowed he, ne'er to tread again
  Green Erin's soil, his glory and his joy,
Till Conal Carnach fetched him o'er the main,
  Or else Cuchullain, or the son of Roy,
Fergus, my dearest.   I these three will test,
And learn by proof which loves King Conor best.'

Then Conor unto Conal signed ; and these
  Stood speaking in a casement far apart :
'Conal, if I should send thee o'er the seas,
  And lo ! on Uladh's soil, through Naisi's heart
The Fates sent darkness, what would happen then ?'
And Conal answered ; 'Deaths of many men !

D 2

'King ! if he fell, of Uladh's sons one half
　　For Naisi's sake should lie ere three days dead,
And for my surety broken.'　With a laugh
　　King Conor fillip'd Conal's cheek, and said,
'Fool ! that canst never understand a jest !
Go hence !　It is not thou that lov'st me best !'

Next, to Cuchullain Conor signed ; then spake ;
　　'Cuchullain ! if I sent thee o'er the sea,
With Usnach's exiled sons a pact to make,
　　And then, despite thy surety given, those Three
Vanished, late-landed ; what would happen then ?'
Cuchullain answered ; 'Deaths of many men !

'For, not alone who wrought that deed accursed,
　　Slaying those Three, should perish by this hand,
But they the impious deed who counselled, first ;
　　And, next the man who issued that command !'
Then Conor frowned :—'What night-mare loads thy
　　　　breast ?
Hence, for thou know'st me not ; nor lov'st me best !'

To Fergus last the royal plotter signed,
　　And made, yet softlier tuned, the self-same quest ;
But he the questioner's meaning nought divined,
　　A Prince whose heart, uncovered as his crest,
Contemned disguise ; suspecting treachery none
Thus answered Fergus, Roy's once sceptred son :

'King, thou, and I, and Usnach's sons must die—
   What matters when, if spotless our good name?
The hand that strikes in daylight I defy;
   If traitor's knife attempts them, for that shame
All Uladh's race shall perish, save alone
The stained, yet guiltless king on Uladh's throne!'

Then Conor caught his hand : 'Thou, sole of all
   Lov'st me! The rest but fear :—they never loved!
Cautious are they : thou swift at honour's call!
   Now therefore be thy love and fealty proved :
To Alba speed : bring home that exiled Three,
Thyself their surety, pledge, and guarantee.

'But with them plight this covenant beside,
   That instant when they tread my kingdom's strand
To me they speed ; with no man else abide ;
   Favour or feast accept at no man's hand :
My bread must be the first those exiles break ;
All griefs thenceforth forgotten for its sake.

'I charge thee too from Alba's coast returned
   To land at Barach's castle in the north ;—
There shall thy monarch's further will be learned :'
   Then Fergus pledged his word, and issued forth :
But Conor beckoned Barach from the feast ;
Then long time stood a-gazing north and east.

Low-toned he spake ; 'Barach ! a keep thou hast
   There where the grey cliffs break the northern brine :
When Fergus comes from Alba, hold him fast :
   Heap high thy banquet ; make that proud one thine !
If from thy board he turns he stands forsworn,
By Geisa bound no good man's feast to scorn.

' But thou, the sons of Usnach send to me :
   What cause I have to trust that race thou knowest :
Be sure thy feast hold out two days or three :
   My love thenceforth thou hast where'er thou goest.'
The courtier smiled, and bowed, 'I hear, and heed :'
And Conor thus ; 'True friend is friend at need !'

Next morning Fergus o'er the waters sped
   At earliest dawn ; with him his sons alone,
Illan the Fair ; Buini the Ruthless Red,
   His shield-bearer, the third.   By swift winds blown
They rushed above the waves a day and night ;
At dawn Loch Etive's mountains loomed in sight.

Ere noon he landed on the Alban coast :
   Wild from the woods a stag there issued bounding ;
The prince his mission grave forgat, and tossed
   Through the green-caverned forest loud-resounding,
As he was ever wont, his hunting cry ;
And lo ! the tents where Naisi dwelt were nigh.

Deirdré and he were playing chess together :
  Their bent heads well nigh met above the board ;
While sunny gleams of that unclouded weather
  Glancing through boughs the chequered ivory scored.
Her brow was bright with thought ; her hand, raised high,
Above-its destined prize hung hoveringly.

The cry of Fergus reached them. Naisi spake ;
  ' Erin ! A son of Erin breathed that shout ! '
Deirdré replied ; ' Not so ! On Etive's lake
  Some fisher boasts a spoil, or chieftain's scout
Welcomes his fellows far away. Play on ! '
She laughed ; but from her cheek the rose was gone.

Once more abroad the cry of Fergus pealed ;
  And Naisi cried : ' Our Erin nursed that voice ! '
Then Deirdré : ' Nay, but from some rock-girt field
  Loud-voiced the shepherd bids his mates rejoice :
Some boar is slain, or wolf that vexed the land ;
Play on ! ' And on her heart she pressed her hand.

But when a third time rang that shout, now nearer,
  The three brave brothers recognised the sound,
And, listening, larger grew their eyes, and clearer,
  And from their seats they leaped, and gazed around,
And smote their palms, and clamoured, ' O the joy !
Fergus is come ! Our Fergus ! Fergus Roy ! '

Then Naisi sent the twain abroad to meet him ;
  But Deirdré said, 'I knew that earliest cry !
Woe to the man, and them this hour who greet him !
  This day the bolt is launched from yonder sky :
This day the Destiny foretold beginneth :
Woe to the Three ! Worst woe to him who sinneth !

' All night I saw three birds from Erin's peaks
  To Alba strain through tempest and eclipse :
Three honey-drops they wafted on their beaks :—
  O Love ! they dropped that sweetness on thy lips ;
Ere long each death-black beak, and crownèd head
With life-blood from thy heart, O Love, was red !'

She rose : on visions dread she seemed to stare !
  She stood : she pressed her hands upon her eyes :
From the wan brows the horror-stricken hair
  Bickering like meteors rose, or seemed to rise ;
She towered aloft a prophetess ; till, near,
The step well known of Fergus smote their ear.

She whispered low : ' Trample the honeyed lure !
  Make not with Conor ! He would have thy blood !'
A moment more, and, entering from the moor,
  Fergus, that royal presence, by them stood :
The cloud fell from her ! Basking like blue sky
She met her husband's guest full lovingly.

There stood they, Fergus loftiest by the head,
　His sons beside him, stalwart men, and tall,
Illan the Fair, Buini the Ruthless Red :
　Reverent and sweet she kissed them, each and all,
She and the Brothers : next they made demand
Of news the latest from their native land.

Swift came the answer ; ' Friends, the news is this ;
　The king repents him of the ignoble deed
That cost his realm her bravest ; zealous is
　To quench that deed, and cancel ; hath decreed
That you and yours, henceforth and evermore
Shall live secure on Erin's sacred shore :

' Likewise of this, a kingdom's oath and pledge,
　I stand myself, surety and guarantee :
Conor in turn, to dull past injury's edge
　Demands, implores a single vow from thee,
That till beside his board thou breakest bread
No meaner house than his shall roof thy head.'

Then Naisi and the brethren rose in joy ;
　But Deirdré came before them speaking thus,
' King—for, except the race and stock of Roy,
　O'er Uladh kings may reign, but not o'er us—
The eagle lives not save in large domain :
My husband won this land, and here must reign !

'King Conor caught and caged me, yet a child ;
   King Conor into exile drave these Three ;
The growing greatness of that race exiled   .
   This day he fears ; and calls them back : but we
Desire a healthier breeze than makes resort
Within the perfumed precinct of a court.'

'Lady, you doubt the safety of your Lord !—
   " Must reign ! "   I reign no more ; not less my name
Would move in might before him like a sword
   Though all the hosts of Erin 'gainst him came ! '
A red spot stood on Fergus' crownless brow ;
The Three looked up ; and spake : ' We go, and now ! '

Then Deirdré inly said ; ' We go to die : '
   Death-pale she stood, yet spake no further word ;
Their promise pledged, albeit unwittingly,
   The worst that might befall them she preferred
To treason's semblance and a vow forsworn :
She spread the feast ; westward they sailed ere morn.

And ever as the wine-dark seas they clave
.   The sons of Usnach stood upon the prow
And spread their arms to Erin o'er the wave ;
   And each to each exclaimed ; ' To guide the plough
Or break the clod, still breathing Erin's air,
Were better than to rule and reign elsewhere ! '

But Deirdré stood upon the vessel's stern,
  Alone, with eyes on Alba's headlands bent,
Dreaming the hills she could no more discern,
  And as they faded thus she made lament,
' O Land, our home no more, to me and mine
Gentle˜thou wert ; therefore my heart is thine !

' O beauteous Land, oft on thy heathery bed,
  Wearied with chase, upon my sleepless heart
My Naisi laid at noon his sleeping head ;
  And therefore thine I am ; and dear thou art.
I came to thee with Naisi hand in hand,
But now no more I see thee, beauteous Land !

' O Coona ! mid thy maiden buds the thrush
  Sang well in spring !   In thee the autumnal berry
Sent forth its flash from reddening brake and bush
  Like scoff from hard old lip of beldam merry !
We laughed to mark it, while far off we heard
Ainli with Ardan sing as bird with bird.

' Glenorchy, O Glenorchy ! sweet in thee
  To hear the cuckoo's note, that glad new-comer ;
And sweet o'er Masan's sands to watch the sea
  Sleep on unwakened half the long, blue summer !
Thou gav'st us, O thou Erin of the East !
The song, the chase, the battle, and the feast !

'Loch Etive, O Loch Etive ! near thy shore,
　　Lulled by thy waters pure, and airs heart-healing,
Latest we lived, who live there now no more ;
　　Earliest in thee we raised our little shieling :—
Good things the sons of Usnach gat from thee,
And I, the ill-omened sister of the Three !'

Thus in her song honouring the land she loved
　　Sad Deirdré stood while back the waters hoar
Streamed from the ship ; and singing never moved :
　　From her chilled lip the wind its music bore,
Till plainly Erin's cliffs at last shone forth,
And Barach's castle facing to the North.

Then Barach, as that fated bark drew near,
　　With courteous seeming but a purpose fell
Sailed forth to meet it, making goodly cheer
　　With bannered boat and tossing coracle
So densely clustered that the billow green
Betwixt them scarcely showed its sparkling sheen.

Ere long the exiles leaped on Erin's strand :
　　The courtier followed fast : with loud-voiced glee
He bade them welcome to their native land,
　　And kissed the hands of each full reverently,
Deirdré's the last ; and said ; 'Your home is here !
Abide a week, and after that a year !'

But when the Brothers told him of their oath
  In no man's house to eat, or rest their head,
Howe'er to slight a friendly welcome loth,
  Until with Conor they had broken bread,
He turned to Fergus ;—' Oath thou too hast sworn
Long since, to pass no friendly feast in scorn.

' Behold, for thee this day my board is decked ;
  My dish is garnished ; and my fatlings slain :
Likewise to greet thee many a chief elect
  Hath sped this day from distant vale and plain :
If vain their zeal, and all that loyal haste
To greet my guest, I stand henceforth disgraced.'

Him Fergus heard, and stood in anguish mute,
  His giant bulk bowed by his spirit's pain
That ever downward worked from scalp to foot :
  Like stag whom serpent folds begin to strain
He stood—that strives in vain that coil to break—
And flame was on his face while thus he spake ;

' Ill done, ill done, O Barach, is thy deed !
  Ill-timed, ill-omened, and unblest thy feast '—
Then Barach ; ' Let those Three to Conor speed ;
  The king is greatest here, and I the least :
But thou—thine oath that later pledge foreran :
If broke, it lays thine honour under ban.'

Still Fergus mused ;—' 'Tis true : that oath I made ;
  Made ere an upstart's craft had filched my crown :
To break it were my greatness to degrade,
  To blot a princely birth, a life's renown :
Uladh would cry ; "He shames the blood of Roy
To 'scape the frown of Nessa's ill-crowned boy !" '

Doubt bred new doubt :—away the False One strode ;
  But Fergus still mused on, and never stirred,
His royal head depressed and neck embowed ;
  At last he turned to Naisi with this word,
' What must I do ? '   But ere her lord replied,
Deirdré spake first, with queenly port and pride :

' The choice is thine, not his ; and this that choice ;
  For a feast's sake to cast from thee thy charge,
Subject and servile to a courtier's voice ;
  Or spurn that feast, and walk, a soul at large.'
And Fergus said ; ' My sons with thine and thee
Might ride.   I bind on them my guarantee.'

Low-toned he spake ; but Naisi heard, and thús
  Made answer, reddening like a rising moon,
' We scorn their aid !   Our swords suffice for us !
  All help beside we count a worthless boon ! '
Then Fergus frowned : At once from doubt released
With them he sent his sons, and joined the feast.

CANTO THE THIRD.

So forth the Brothers rode, while high o'erhead
  Through that primeval forest's woven screen
Now in long lanes the sky its radiance shed,
  And now in purple stars of splendour keen ;
Nor far behind them marched the Usnach clan,
Loud singing and on trampling like one man.

But Deirdré slowly lifting eyes divine,
  Dewed with dark tears, upon the Brothers, spake ;
' True counsel, lo ! I give you, brothers mine ;
  And yet that counsel true ye will not take ;
There shine the rocks of Rathlin ! On its shore
Abide till this disastrous feast is o'er ! '

Then spake to Illan, Fergus' kindlier son,
  The Ruthless Red ; 'Small faith in us they place !'
Whom Naisi hearing, made reply, 'Ride on :'
  And Deirdré raised to heaven her heaven-sweet face,
And made this song ; for, as in girlhood, all
Her musings, dark or bright, grew musical.

'O would my Love were safe in some far isle,
  And I were like some shadow passed away ;
Yea, though some other liegeful wife, the while,
  Partook his board at eve, his chase by day :
For I am that doomed Babe of long ago ;
And I on those fair Three have brought this woe !

'One time by far Loch Etive—'twas in jest—
  My Naisi kissed a sweet-eyed Alban maid :
I sought my death ! my bark from crest to crest
  I dashed, too deeply wounded to upbraid !
The Brothers saw, and followed fast—and I—
Ah, that for me those peerless Three should die ! '

Meanwhile all day in light discourse or deep
  The sons of Usnach and of Fergus rode,
And came at eve to Fuad's mountain-steep ;
  But Deirdré, bent for once by sorrow's load
Though strong, behind them dropped, and on a bank
Moon-lit sat down ; and slumber on her sank.

There Naisi found her 'neath a yew-tree old,
  Shivering ; and she his steps approaching knew
Though sleeping still ; and through the moonlight cold
  T'wards him stretched forth her hand so kind and true;
And, 'What, O what is this,' he said, ' My Queen ? '
Wak'ning she answered, anguished yet serene :

'A dream it was that kept me from thy side :
  Wakeful all day that dream I saw, and see :
I saw great Fergus' sons beside us ride,
  Brothers in blood ; disjoined in destiny :
Illan a bleeding bulk without a head,
I saw : yet true he proved when traitors fled.

'Buini I saw, the Ruthless Red ; full strong
  He towered, and stately as a summer tree :
But, when that strife dishonest did us wrong,
  No help he proved, O Love, to thine and thee !
So one was faithful, yet of greatness shorn :
And one was greatness perjured and forsworn.

'Now ride we on !' they rode for many an hour,
  Till, through an oak-glade in that glimmering wood,
They saw Emania, veiled in cloud and shower :
  Above the edge of that black cloud there stood
A moon nigh setting in a sanguine shroud ;
And many thunders heard they, far, not loud.

Upon that sanguine shroud as on a sign
  Deirdré gazed long ; then turned her eyes, and spake :
'True counsel, lo ! I give you, brothers mine,
  And yet that counsel true ye will not take ;
No further t'wards Emania ride this hour ;
Seek we, not far it stands, Cuchulain's tower !

' Or house with Conal Carnach, leal and true :
    He to the court ere noon with us will ride—
Naisi ! when on that causeway I and you
    That evening sang, what prayer hadst thou denied ?'
Yet, though she chid him, nearer him she crept :
The one sole time that in his arms she wept !

Buini drew near !   At once the Three replied,
    ' Because we never feared and cannot fear
To Eman on we will whate'er betide ! '
    Unseen by him she wiped away her tear ;
While from the black boughs fell a poison-dew ;
And Fate her net more closely round them drew.

Thenceforth was Deirdré changed.   To Eman's gate
    They rode, and thrice beneath it blew their horn :
Indifferent, yea, as one with either fate
    Alike content, she spake in careless scorn ;
' Omens the Druids find in bird and beast :
A Druid I ; a laughing one at least !

' I doubted Conor's faith : if mine the fault
    Harbouring distrust, King Conor thus will speak :
" Abide with me three months : partake my salt ;
    Drink of my cup ; my bread securely break ! "
If under alien roof he bids us lie
Then know his pit is dug ; and we shall die.'

She spake ! around her lip a smile there curled ;
　　Her kindling eye was fixed as eye of one
Who sees, beyond the limits of the world,
　　Beyond the thresholds of our moon and sun,
Beyond the abysmal night, a gleam of day,
And can abide the issue come what may.

As thus they stood the gates were opened wide ;
　　Anon forth stepped a herald with this word,
' Great Sirs, the King, himself by sickness tried,
　　Within the Red-Branch House hath decked your
　　　　board
With Uladh's best, from mead and river brought : '
They on each other gazed, yet answered nought.

' He bids you there with blessing.' At that speech
　　Silent they sought that House.　In stately throng
The knights received them : yet on brows of each
　　Devoid of guile, a dubious sadness clung :
Not less the seats were set ; the tables spread :
Nor ceased that revel till the day was sped.

Not all partook it.　Silent and apart
　　In a huge window caverned from the wall
By some high builder's long-forgotten art,
　　Sat Deirdré, and the Brothers three.　No thrall

E 2

To royal craft the warriors now.   What meant
The king, they knew, and waited the event.

Scorning to make complaint, they scorned not less
     To share a traitor's feast, and ate of nought,
Waving each dish away in haughtiness,
     Save little loaves that with them they had brought.
Their chess-board next they ranged with pawn and queen;
And Deirdré laughed or frowned the moves between.

Meantime with Levarcam King Conor spake ;
     ' Forth, since I spared thy life when Deirdré fled,
And tidings bring me whether, for love's sake,
     Yet lives her beauty on that False One's head :
The girl hath known rough skies and scanty board : '
Then Levarcam went forth, with wiles well stored.

Drawing a thousand thoughts into one noose
     Of woman-craft she sped, in silks arrayed ;
And came with speed, such speed as age may use,
     To where at chess the sentenced princes played
In that high window ; next one finger raised
High as her brow ; then round her peering gazed.

Naisi she loved from childhood ; loved scarce less
     His brothers ; felt for Deirdré love and spleen :—
' Through grace of yours, all-bashful Forwardness,
     Save for my craft this trunk had headless been !

I wiled the sword from Conor's hand !   Well, well !
My Wanton's face retains its childish spell !

' I come to you at peril of my life—
   Hush, hush ! place hand on lip !   They must not
      hear !
With rumours dark Emania's streets are rife :
   The king has vowed your death :—draws any near ?
Then when the Babe was born, the seer foretold—
What ?   Must men die because a maid was bold ? '

In tears awhile the faded fine one stood ;
   And next, mechanic-wise oracular,
Kept nodding of her head.   Then changed her mood
   To fires of youth.   'Close gate, and casement bar !
Fight well, ye sons of Fergus !   If your sire
Makes speed, he'll trample down this flame in mire !'

Last, like that bird which fan-like spreads her plumes
   For pride, to Conor's palace she returned,
And found him seated in presageful glooms ;
   And cried as though some reptile shape she spurned,
'Woe, woe ; for Deirdré's brightness is gone by ;—
Brown moth is she that once was butterfly ! '

King Conor heard, ill-pleased, and yet well-pleased,
   And stood, before him dangling still this thought
At least then Naisi of his love is eased ;
   And that proud minx has lost my realm for nought :

Perhaps 'twere best to let old rancours pass :
Kingdoms live on ; but beauty fades like grass.

Thus mused the king : but while he sat at meat
    And, later, when the wine had fired his blood,
The thought of Deirdré's face, tender and sweet,
    Too bright to fade, star-like before him stood :
And loud he cried : 'Sits any brave man here
Who dreads not death, and holds King Conor dear ?

' Forth to the Red-Branch Mansion let him speed,
    And there with Deirdré secret converse hold,
And learn if yet upon her lives indeed
    The glory of that beauty hers of old.'
Then Trendorn went, a sordid churl, ill-starred,
And found that mansion's gateways closed and barred :

Yet clomb he darkling, to that casement high ;
    And Deirdré turned her face :—in awe and fear
Of that great splendour o'er it shed, the spy
    Slid from his place, and, racing like a deer,
To Conor cried ; 'As shines in heaven the sun,
So she on earth : and like her there is none !'

That instant Conor saw the maid again !
    That instant rage of love his heart possessed
Venomed by past repulse, and jealous pain :
    And thus he cried, hoarse-voiced with stifling breast,

'Storm ye the Red-Branch House ! Die, he that will !
Mine was that maid : and mine I deem her still.'

In silence sat the chiefs, mindful at once
    Of duty sworn to Uladh's king, their Lord,
And of his counter-pledge to Usnach's sons ;
    But all the Bonachts ranged adown the board
Rushed forth to boast their zeal, and clutch their prey,
Aliens base-born that fought not save for pay.

To these were joined the vile ones of the street ;
    For in their breasts Conor this seed had sown,
Imposture sordid, and obscene conceit,
    ' Traitors, in Alba late to princes grown,
Would make their Pictish tyrant Uladh's king ! '
They girt the Red-Branch House, thus clamouring.

Long time in silence stood, and sore amazed,
    Those brave but simple knights o'er Erin feared :
For Usnach's sons as kings they prized and praised ;
    But like a God King Conor they revered :
At last they spake, and after that changed not,
' We in this war will bear nor part, nor lot.'

And when the stony storm blackened the heaven,
    And gate rolled in, and casement burst and brake,
And all that House was as a ship rock-riven,
    In midnight storm, they sat, and never spake ;

For two contrarient thoughts their minds had cleft—
Astonied men of manhood's might bereft.

Naisi, meantime, and Deirdré, fixed, attent,
   Their eyes in stillness on the ivory board,
And silent o'er their game the brothers bent ;
   But Fergus' sons stood up with hand on sword,
Forth from the casement gazing ; and the red
Burned on their brows : then Deirdré, careless, said,

' Long time, methinks, at feast doth Fergus tarry—
   Good speed for that crowned hawk which hangs on
      high
With beak turned downward t'ward his skiey quarry ! '
   Buini broke in ; ' My sire is false ; not I ! '
And gat him down ; and shouted Fergus' name :
And straight a host around him flocking came.

But Conor sent for Buini, and at door
   Whispered him low ; ' I yield thee Fo-äd-Fell ! '
Yet Buini spurned the bribe, and said ; 'What more ?'
   And Conor thus ; ' Henceforth mine oracle
At council board be thou, and only thou ! '
Then Buini pledged with Conor hand and vow.

Thenceforth around the Red-Branch Mansion higher
   The madness of the people surged, and roar
As though of tempest when great woods catch fire,
   Or winter waves raking some northern shore ;

And on the portals seven they dashed ; and lo !
Their mighty hinges groaned 'neath blow on blow.

Meantime the Red-Branch Knights, like men in sleep
    Trod the vast courts ; or like some shepherd boor
Who feels his way on cliffs that crest the deep
    When mist invests the mountain and the moor ;
Or stood and gazed from far on Deirdré's brow—
Strong knights of old ; men ineffectual now.

Then Deirdré, as the battle raged below,
    Spake lightly thus, while on she pushed a pawn,
' Buini has gone like Fergus—let him go ! '
    But Illan, grieved at heart, with sword half drawn,
Replied, ' While lives this sword, whoe'er may fly,
Faithful and true to Usnach's Sons am I ! '

And gat him down, and drew a host, and drave
    Southward that seething mass a mile and more,
As when the wind before it drives the wave ;
    And shouted, ' traitors ' still ; and slew six score.
Then—sped from heaven—above the heads of all
Ran Fear ; and reached King Conor's council-hall.

There, girt by chiefs sat Conor on his throne
    With cloudy brows, and pale lips ridged in scorn,
Who thus addressed Fiacre, his first-born son ;
    ' Son, thou and he the self-same hour were born,

Illan—the man that from this head even now
Sweeps Uladh's crown !   Go forth and meet him, thou !

'And, since the arms he weareth of his sire,
    Fergus, once king, wear thou mine arms this day,
"Ocean," my shield, that sea-like roars in ire
    Echoed on Erin's farthest coasts, men say ;
And "Victory's wing," and "Flying Fate," my spears
And "Death," my sword, annealed in widows' tears.'

Then strode Fiacre to battle, iron-mailed :
    But straight the king to Conal Carnach sent,
'My kingdom reels by rebel hosts assailed :
    My son goes forth to meet them.   Sickness-bent
I wait the close.   My bravest knight, my best !
Strike for thy king !   What care I for the rest ? '

Next to Cuchullain sent he : but that knight
    Frowned on the herald in his perilous mood,
And said ; 'What part have I in civil fight ? '
    Soon, face to face Fiacre and Illan stood :
At last the royal youth, 'neath Illan's sword
Sank to one knee : at once in fury roared—

Thus much and more the legends old avouch—
    'Ocean,' King Conor's shield ; for wroth was he
A prince's head beneath his shade should crouch,
    And wroth Emania's coming doom to see :

Three times the shield sent forth that sea-like roar ;
And thrice the three chief waves on Erin's shore

Responded, from the blue deeps landward rolling ;
   The wave of Toth on Erin's northern coast ;
Green Clidna's wave like funeral bells far tolling ;
   And Rory's wave, the loudest.   Through the host
Rushed Conal Carnach at the third wave's cry,
And, shouting thus, ' King Conor's son will die ! '

In dashed while Illan o'er Fiacre was bending—
   Illan his friend—and drave through Illan's side,
Knowing him not, the sword, his heart-strings rending :
   But Illan rose, and spake before he died :
' Thy deeds were great, O friend ! This last—this one—
Was not like Conal !   I am Fergus' son !

' I die to guard his name and Conor's pledge.'
   Then Conal cried in storm of rage and woe,
' Since Conor lied to me this faulchion's edge
   Shall pay the debt he owes, and that I owe,
A death to honour and to vengeance due ; '
And down he dragged Fiacre, and, trampling, slew.

That hour the royal host pierced through by grief,
   Clamoured, yet quailed at glance of Conal's eye ;
While shouted Illan's band, ' Be thou our chief !
   Illan is dead.'   Vouchsafing no reply

Silent from both he turned ; and, like a God
Spurning some death-doomed city, homeward strode.

But when the tidings came, ' Fiacre is dead,'
    King Conor dropped in swoon ; and if that hour
Illan had lived, and not the Ruthless Red,
    All Eman's chiefs had joined to his their power ;
For Illan, like his sire, had Eman's love :—
Thus Fate round Usnach's Sons her net enwove.

Around the Red-Branch House that Bonacht host
    Gathered once more : but on the left the might
Of Ardan backward hurled them and their boast ;
    And Ainli's strength rebuked them on the right :
Till came to Conor's heart a wingèd thought ;
And 'Fire !' he cried ; and branch and beam were
      brought,

Circling the walls : up rushed the red flames roaring ;
    And one by one, the seven great gates fell down ;
Then rushed from court to court, still onward pouring,
    Native with alien, man-at-arms with clown :
Yet still the assailed fought on from stair to stair,
Long time in rage, and later in despair.

Meanwhile along the loftier cloister floors
    As though with fettered feet moved knight with knight,
Or, idiot-like, stood peering by the doors,
    Divided purpose making null their might ;

Or stood in groups, and watched where, undismayed,
That haughty pair at chess in silence played.

But Naisi, glancing up, on Deirdré's hair
   Saw the fierce reflex from a roof far off,
And on her marble cheek the fiery glare,
   And heard from her fine lip the careless scoff,
'At Conor's fireside welcome sits the guest !'—
He rose, and sudden clasped her to his breast ;

Then held her from him, on her countenance bright
   Gazing.   In neither face that hour was fear :
She saw in his a sadness infinite :
   He saw, in hers, content, and princely cheer.
At last she spake ; 'Self-questioning thoughts repel,
Nor grieve at trust misplaced ; for all is well !

'O Love, not thus upon that causeway old
   We stood that day, chaunting our nuptials high !
Yet nothing is that was not then foretold—
   Hast thou not happy been ?   More happy I,
That hour thy love ; for three glad years thy bride ;
That ran, and slept, and wakened at thy side !

'The good must still the auspice be of good ;
   They never loved who dream that Love can
      die !
In lordlier strength, in happier sanctitude
   Be sure he waits us in some realm more high.

All thanks, thou Power Unknown !' She spake and
    kissed
With all her young bright face her husband's breast.

Then rushed to them the Brothers shouting, ' Forth !'
    And forth they sped through courts foot deep in
      blood,
And reached the gate that issued to the north
    Where fierceliest raged the fight : and Deirdré trod
Midmost between the twain, and Naisi first ;
And on the battle lion-like they burst.

And still the Three above their sister raised
    Their mighty shields that, like three glittering spheres
Glared through the gloom, and friend and foeman
      dazed ;
    And fierce as living creatures worked their spears
Dealing the death around, till all the plain
Lay like a death-vault, strewn by warriors slain.

And, foot by foot, the hostile hosts fell back ;
    And, more and more, true friends, till then dismayed,
Fought by their side, or followed in their track :
    Due northward t'ward the sea their march they made :
And, marching, eyed full oft that fortress fired—
Therein full many a Red-Branch Knight expired.

Then, as a poplar near a river whitens
   By gusts o'er-blown, and as some snowy vale
Grows grimly dark when sudden o'er it brightens
   The mountain's moonlit flank, thus dark, thus pale,
Grew Conor with far eyes their course pursuing ;
' They 'scape,' he cried, ' and that is my undoing !

' Cathbad ! give ear ! '—for by him stood that hour
   The blind old Druid with the silver hair—
' To Alba make they; thence ere long with power
   Return in vengeance ! Think you they will spare ?
And Conal and Cuchullain by their side
Will march ; and Fergus ! Would that I had died !

' Help, Cathbad ! last of friends ! If e'er from thee
   Or child or stripling, help or love I gat ;
My craft has futile proved : my legions flee ;
   Yet magic power, we know, can level flat
All power of man in one brief moment's space :
Slay me, or spare my kingdom this disgrace ! '

To whom replied the old man tremulously,
   ' Would God that ne'er had come that night of old
When shriek on shriek confused the revelry,
   And I that new-born Infant's fate foretold ;
For ne'er in ninety years deceived was I
Or by man's art, or wiles of Destiny !

'Not less, great king, this deed I dare not do,
  For Justice keeps an axe, and keen its edge,
In worlds unseen ; and they their sin shall rue
  Who spill the righteous blood, or break the pledge.
Here Wrong holds court ; but Justice reigneth there :—
King !   In those unseen regions I have share !'

Him Conor answered : 'Cathbad ! oath I make
  By all those regions sacred and unseen,
By all the Powers that in them sleep or wake,
  The Gods that are, or shall be, or have been,
This hand on Usnach's sons shall work no wrong ;
Captive, not dead, I wish them—nor for long.'

He spake, and softly to the Druid stept
  And pressed that Druid's hand to lips and eyes ;
Then o'er the old man's heart compassion crept,
  With flatter'd pride, which oft to good and wise
Makes way, thus veiled, in weak, unwary hour ;
And o'er the North he waved his wand of power.

Three times with muttered spell he waved that wand,
  Filling the air with visions of dismay :
That hour through Conor's host, and far beyond,
  Usnach's brave clan had carved its desperate way ;
Yet, galled and broken, hung upon their rear
That Bonacht swarm.   It raged, but came not near.

On Usnach's clan the Druid's spells took hold,
　　Feigning what was not : and the wide green plain
Seemed to their eyes a great flood slowly rolled
　　From phantom hills.　Through it they pushed with
　　　　pain :
And on their eyes a phantom mist was driven :
And o'er them leaned, low-hung, a phantom heaven.

But, forward as they toiled, that flood ere long
　　Deepened, so seemed it, to a billowy sea ;
And they, with arms in swimmer's act forth flung,
　　Clave that imagined deep.　Alone the Three
And Deirdré, spite of spells, illusion-proof,
Saw still green field, and heaven's unclouded roof.

Ah God !　How oft in agony that hour
　　Caught they this man and that, and cried, 'Arise !
But now triumphant, will ye crouch and cower
　　In death the coward's jest, the traitor's prize ?'
'Twas vain !　Those dreamers still swam on till brand
And shield down dropt from every helpless hand.

The Bonachts stood in marvel ; then dashed on,
　　Their terror past ; and Conor sent decree,
' Except the woman, see ye spare not one !
　　Smite first the sons of Usnach, smite the Three !'

F

And lo ! like sheep that old and far-famed clan
Lay on the war-field, slaughtered to a man.

Alone, girt round by hostile rank on rank,
 Usnach's great sons, unvanquished, still fought on ;
And ever when their arms exhausted sank,
 And for a moment strength was all but gone,
Deirdré, amidst them, like a prophet poured
Her war-songs forth, and still their strength restored.

'Twas vain !   At noon the direful battle ceased :
 That glorious Three who late the world o'er-strode
Lay facing to the South, and West, and East ;
 A frozen spectre Deirdré o'er them stood :
The Bonachts gat their hire :—kneeling drew near
Uladh's sad sons, with many a moan and tear.

Remembering days gone by, the victors there
 Wept for the dead : and when the king sent word
To leave those Three unburied, stark and bare
 For beasts to rend, his mandate they abhorred,
And dug the grave where those brave Brothers died :
And, reverent, therein laid them, side by side.

Upon the right of that dim burial pit
 Was Conal Carnach standing ; on its left
Cuchullain ; each with brows in sorrow knit,
 Each with a heart by one sharp memory cleft :

For true to Usnach's sons in word and deed
These twain had lived ; yet failed them at their need.

But Deirdré at the grave-head stood alone,
    The surging crowd held back by holy dread ;
Her face was white as monumental stone ;
    Her hands, her garb, from throat to foot were red
With blood—their blood.   Standing on life's dark verge
She scorned to die till she had sung their dirge.

' Dead are the eagles three of Culan's peaks ;
    The lions three of Uladh's forest glades ;
The wonders three of Alba's lakes and creeks ;
    The loved ones three of Etive's fair young maids :
The crownless sons of Erin's Throne are sped :
The glories of the Red Branch Order dead.

' Is there who dreams that, now my Naisi's breath
    Is stilled, his wife will tarry from his side ?
Thou man that mak'st far down yon cave of death,
    Be sure thou dig it deep, and dig it wide !
There lie the Brothers Three !   'Tis just, 'tis meet
Their Sister take her place before their feet.

' Ofttimes for me they piled their shields and spears
    In Alba's woods, roofing my winter bed :
Thou man that build'st, this day, far down their biers,
    Be sure the spear and shield are nigh the head !

F 2

They had great joy in these of old : below
Lack them they shall not, though they meet no foe.

'Ofttimes I heard in Etive's hunting grounds
    Their deep-toned voices rolling like the sea—
My Naisi led me from our native bounds :
    Ainli and Ardan followed.   Woe is me !
That hour when I was born I should have died :
The ill-omened Infant was the ill-omened Bride !'

Thus Deirdré sang, and silent stood a space ;
    Then spake once more : 'I come, my Love, my Lord !'
And forward fell into that loved embrace,
    In happy death to him she loved restored :
When Conal and Cuchullain raised her head :
There lay she smiling, dead among the dead.

The men of Erin reared the funeral stone,
    And piled the cairn, in Ogham characters
Cyphering the sorrows of the Four thereon :
    And, age by age, that legend grey avers,
Sad voices issuing from that grave foretold
The fates of lovers young and kingdoms old.

But Cathbad laid a curse upon the king,
    Likewise his race : and Eman, and the land,
Because they hated not that evil thing,
    And hindered not, with dreadful rites he banned ;

And lastly, 'Woe to me not less,' he cried,
Three times ; and gat him to his place ; and died.

With speed came up at earliest gleam of morn
   Fergus to Eman.   Dreadful his array ;
For many a chief, though Conor's liegeman sworn,
   In wrath had joined the old king on his way :
And Fergus cursed the Ruthless Red, and said.
'A woman's hand one day shall strike him dead !

The battle ceased not till that day was done :
   With his own hand, at noontide, Fergus slew
Maini, King Conor's last surviving son :
   Old Eman's walls and towers to earth he threw ;
And burned the city.   Half the men therein
Perished, and many an infant, for its sin.

THE CHILDREN OF LIR

AN ANCIENT IRISH ROMANCE

'Deus dedit carmina in nocte'—JOB, cap. xxxv. v. 10

TO THE MEMORY OF

DENIS FLORENCE MAC-CARTHY,

TO WHOM ENGLISH AND IRISH READERS OWE,

BESIDE MANY A GAELIC LEGEND,

THE BEST WORKS OF CALDERON,

THIS POEM

IS DEDICATED.

THE CHILDREN OF LIR.

CANTO THE FIRST.

ERE yet great Miledh's sons to Erin came,
  Lords of the Gael, Milesian styled more late,
An earlier tribe, Tuatha was their name,
  Likewise Dedannan, ruled the Isle of Fate,
A tribe that knew nor clan, nor priest, nor bard,
Wild as the waves, and as the sea-cliffs hard.

Some say that race of old from Greece exiled
  Long time had sojourned in the frozen North
Roaming Norwegian wood and Danish wild :
  To Erin thence more late they issued forth,
And thither brought two gifts both loved and feared,
The ' Lia Fail,' and Ogham lore revered.

Fiercer they were, not manlier, than the Gael,
  Large-handed, swift of foot, dark-haired, dark-eyed,
With sudden gleams athwart their faces pale,
  Transits of fancies swift, or angry pride :

Strange lore they boasted, imped by insight keen ;
Blackened at times by gusts of causeless spleen.

These, when the white fleet of the Gael drew nigh
   Green Erin's shore, their heritage decreed,
O'er-meshed, through rites unholy, earth and sky
   With sudden gloom.   The invaders took no heed,
But dashed through dark their galleys on the strand ;
Then clapped their hands, and laughing leaped to land.

Around them flocked Tuatha's race in guile,
   Unarmed, with mocking voice and furtive mien,
And scoffed : ' Not thus your fathers fought erewhile !
   Say, call ye warriors knaves that creep unseen,
While true men sleep, up inlet dim, and fiord,
Filching the land they proved not with their sword ? '

Then to the Gael their bard, Amergin, spake :
   ' Sail forth, my sons, nine waves across the deep,
And when this island-race are armed, come back ;
   Take then their realm by force ; and, taking, keep ! '
The Gael sailed forth, nine waves ; then turned, and gazed—
Night wrapt the isle, and storm by magic raised !

Round Erin's shores like leaves their ships were blown :
   Strewn on her reefs lay bard and warrior drowned :
Not less the Gael upreared ere long that throne
   Two thousand years through all the West renowned.

O'er Taillten's field God held the scales of Fate :
That last dread battle closed the dire debate.

There fell those three Tuatha queens who gave
   The land their names—they fell by death discrowned : [1]
There many a Gaelic chieftain found his grave :
   Thenceforth the races twain adjusted bound
And right, at times by league, at times by war ;
Nor any reigned as yet from shore to shore.

Still here and there Tuatha princes ruled
   Now in green vale, and now on pale blue coast,
A warrior one, and one in magic schooled ;
   The graver made Druidic lore their boast,
And knew the secret might of star and leaf :
Grey-haired King Bove stood up of these the chief.

Southward by broad Lough Derg his palace stood :
   Northward, beside Emania's lonely mere,
In Finnahá, embowered mid lawn and wood,
   King Lir abode, a warrior, not a seer ;
Well loved was he, plain man with great, true heart,
Who loathed, despite his race, the sorcerer's art.

Five centuries lived he ere that better light
   Gladdened the earth from Bethlehem : ne'ertheless
He judged his land with justice and with might,
   Tempering the same at times with gentleness ;

     [1] Bamba, Fodhla, and Eire.

And gave the poor their due ; and made proclaim,
' Let no man smite the old ; the virgin shame.'

His prime was spent in wars : in middle life
 He bade a youthful princess share his throne :
Nor e'er had monarch yet a truer wife
 With tenderer palm or voice of sweeter tone :
The one sole lady of that race was she
Sun-haired, with large eyes azure as the sea.

She moved amid the crafty as a child ;
 Amid the lawless, chaste as unsunned maid ;
Amid the unsparing, as a turtle mild ;
 Wondering at wrong ; too gentle to upbraid :
Yet many a fell resolve, as she rode by,
Died at its birth—the ill-thinker knew not why !

Sadness before her fled : in years long past
 As on a cliff the warriors sang their songs
A harper maid, with eyes that stared aghast,
 Had chaunted, ' Not to us this isle belongs !
The Fates reserve it for a race more true,
Ye children of Dedannan's stock, than you !'

And since she scorned her music to abate,
 Nor ceased to freeze their triumph with her dirge,
The princes and the people rose in hate
 And hurled her harp and her into the surge :

Yet still, halfway 'twixt midnight and the morn,
That dirge swelled up, by tempest onward borne !

Remembering oft this spectre of his youth
   King Lir would sit, a frown upon his brow :
Then came the queen with words of peace and truth ;
   ' Mourn they that sinned !   A child that hour wert thou!
Thou rul'st this land to-day : in years to be
Who best deserves shall wield her sovereignty.'

Then would the monarch doff his sullen mood
   With kingly joy, and, bright as May-day's morn,
Ride forth amid his hounds through wild and wood,
   Thrilling far glens with echoes of his horn ;
Or meet the land's invaders face to face
Well pleased, and homeward hew them with disgrace.

Thus happy lived the pair, and happier far
   When four fair children graced the royal house,
Fairer than flowers, more bright than moon or star
   Shining through vista long of forest boughs.
Finola was the eldest, eight years old :
The yearling, Conn, best loved of all that fold.

These beauteous creatures with their mother shared
   Alike her blissful nature and sweet looks,
Like her swan-soft, swan-white, blue-eyed, bright-haired,
   With voices musical as birds or brooks :

Beings they seemed reserved for some great fate,
Mysterious, high, elect, and separate.

At times they gambolled in the sunny sheen ;
    At times, Fiacre and Aodh at her side,
Finōla paced the high-arched alleys green,
    At once their youthful playmate and their guide :
A mother-hearted child she walked, and pressed
That infant, daily heavier, to her breast.

Great power of Love that, wide as heaven, dost brood
    O'er all the earth, and doest all things well !
Light of the wise, and safeguard of the good !
    Nowhere, methinks, thou better lov'st to dwell
Than in the hearts of innocents that still,
By dangerous love untempted, work Love's will !

Thou shalt be with them when the sleet-wind blows
    Not less than in the violet-braided bower :
Through thee the desert sands shall bud the rose,
    The wild wave anthems sing !   In grief's worst hour
A germ of thine shall breed that quenchless Faith
Amaranth of life, and asphodel of death.

Ah lot of man !   Ah world whose life is change !
    Ah sheer descent from topmost height of good
To deepest gulf of anguish sudden and strange !
    A nation round their monarch's gateway stood :

All day there stood they, whispering in great dread :
The herald came at last—'The Queen is dead !'

In silence still they stood an hour and more,
   Till through the West had sunk the great red sun,
And from the castle wall and turrets hoar
   The latest crimson utterly had gone :
At last the truth had reached them ! then on high
An orphaned People hurled its funeral cry.

They hurled it forth again and yet again,
   The dreadful wont of that barbaric time ;
Cry after cry that reached the far off main,
   And, echoing, seemed from cloud to cloud to climb ;
Then lifted hands like creatures broken-hearted,
Or sentenced men ; and homeward, mute, departed.

Fast-speeding Time, albeit the wounded wing
   He may not bind, brings us at least the crutch ;—
Winter was over, and the on-flying Spring
   Grazed the sad monarch's brow with heavenly touch,
And raised the head, now whitening, from the ground,
And stanched, not healed, the heart's eternal wound.

King Bove, chief sovereign of the dark-haired race,
   Sent to him saying, ' Quit thee like a man !
The Gaels, our scourge, and Erin's sore disgrace,
   Advance, each day, their armies, clan on clan :

Against them march thy host with mine, and take
To wife my daughter, for thy children's sake.'

Lir sadly mused ; but answered : ' Let it be !'
   And drave with fifty chariots in array
To where the land's chief river like a sea,
   There named Lough Derg, spreads out in gulf and bay
And many a woody mountain sees its face
Imaged in that clear flood with softened grace.

There with King Bove the widowed man abode
   Two days amid great feastings.   On the third
The king led forth his daughter—o'er her glowed
   A dim veil jewel-tissued—with this word :
' Behold thy wife !   The world proclaims her fair :
I know her strong to love, and strong to dare.'

And Lir made answer : ' Fair she is as when
   A mist-veiled yew, red-berried, stands in state :
Can love, you say !   Love she my babes ! and then
   With her my love shall bide ; if not—my hate
And she, a crimson on her dusky brow,
Replied, ' If so it be, then be it so !'

King Lir, a fortnight more in revels spent,
   Made journey to his castle in the North
With her, his youthful consort, well content.
   Arrived, in rapture of their loving mirth

Forth rushed into his arms his children four
Bright as those wavelets on their blue lake's shore ;—

On whom the new queen cast a glance oblique
   One moment's space ; then, flinging wide her arms,
With instinct changed, and impulse lightning-like,
   Clasped them in turn and wondered at their charms,
And cried, ' If e'er a stepmother could love
I of that tribe renowned will tenderest prove.'

And so by her great loving of those four
   Still from her husband won she praises sweet
And plaudits from his people more and more ;
   Her own she called them : nor was this deceit :
She loved them with a fitful love—a will
To make them or to mar, for good or ill.

She wooed them still with shows, with flowers, with
      fruit ;
   Daily for them new sports she sought and found :
Yet, if their father praised them, she was mute,
   And, when he placed them on his knee, she frowned,
Murmuring, ' How blue their eyes ! their cheek how
      pale !
Their voices too are voices of the Gael !

Meantime, as month by month in grace they grew,
　　Their father loved them better than before ;
And so, one eve, their slender cots he drew
　　Each from its place remote, and lightly bore,
And laid them ranged before his royal bed ;
And o'er the four a veil gold-woven spread ;

Their mother's bridal-veil: and still as dawn
　　Was in its glittering tissue caged and caught
He left his couch, and, that light veil withdrawn,
　　Before his children stood in silent thought ;
And, if they slept, he kissed them in their sleep,
Then watched them with clasped hands in musings
　　　　deep.

And, if they slept not, from their balmy nest
　　With under-sliding arms he raised them high,
And clasped them each, successive, to his breast,
　　Or on them flashed the first light from the sky :
Then laid him by his mute, sleep-feigning bride,
And slept once more : and oft in sleep he sighed.

Which things abhorring, she her face averse
　　Turned all day steadfast from the astonished throng:
And next, as one that broods upon a curse,
　　She sat in her sick-chamber three weeks long,
And never raised her eyes, nor made complaint,
Dark as a fiend and silent as a saint.

Lastly to Lir she spake : 'Daily I sink
   Downward to death.   I wither in my prime :
Home to my father I would speed, and drink
   Once more the breezes of my native clime.
All night in sleep along Lough Derg I strayed,
And wings of strength about my shoulders played.

'These four—thy children—with me I will take
   To please my father's eye ; he loves them well :
Thou too, whene'er thy leisure serves, shalt make
   Thither thy journey.'   All the powers of Hell
Thrilled at that speech in penal vaults below :
But Lir, no fraud suspecting, answered, ' Go ! '

Therefore next morn when earliest sunrise smote
   Green mead to golden near the full-fed stream,
They caught four steeds that grazed thereby remote,
   And yoked abreast beside the chariot beam ;
And when the sun was sinking toward the West
By Darvra's lake drew rein, and made their rest.

Then the bad queen, descending, round her cast
   A baleful look of mingled hate and woe,
And with those babes into a thicket passed,
   And drew a dagger from her breast ; and lo !
She struck them not, but only wailed and wailed—
In her so strongly womanhood prevailed.

The mood was changed.   She smiled that smile which
    none
·How wise soe'er, beholding, could resist,
And drew those children to her, one by one ;
    Then wailed once more, and last their foreheads
    kissed,
And cried with finger pointing to the lake,
' Hence ! and in that clear bath your pastime take ! '

She spoke, and from their silken garb forth-sliding,
    Ere long those babes were sporting in the bay :
And, as it chanced, the eddy past them gliding
    Wafted a swan's plume : 'twas less white than they :
Frowning, the queen beheld them, and on high
Waved thrice her Druid wand athwart the sky :

Then, standing on the marge wan-cheeked, wide-eyed,
    As near they drew, awe-struck and wondering,
Therewith she smote their golden heads, and cried,
    ' Fly hence, ye pale-faced children of the king !
Cleave the blue mere, or on through ether sail ;
No more his loved ones, but a dolorous tale ! '

Straightway to snow-white swans those children turned :
    And, sideway as they swerved the creatures four
Fixed on her looks with human grief that yearned ;
    Then slowly drifted backward from the shore ;
While loud with voice unchanged, Finola cried,
' Bad deed is thine, false queen and bitter bride !

' Bad deed afflicting babes that harmed thee not ;
　Bad deed, and to thyself an evil dower :
Disastrous more than ours shall be thy lot !
　Thou too shalt feel the weight of Druid power :
From age to age thy penance ne'er shall cease :
Our doom, though long it lasts, shall end in peace.'

Then rang a wild shriek from that dreadful shape :
　' Long, long, aye long shall last those years of woe !
Here on this lake from misty cape to cape
　Three centuries ye shall wander to and fro ;
Three centuries more shall stem with heavier toil
Far Alba's waves, the black sea-strait [1] of Moyle.

' Lastly three centuries where the Eagle-Crest [2]
　O'er-looks the western deep, and Inisglaire,
Upon the mountain waves that know not rest
　Shall be your rolling palace, foul or fair,
Till comes the Tailkenn,[3] sent to sound the knell
Of darkness, and ye hear his Christian bell.'

Lo, as a band of lilies, white and tall
　Beneath a breeze of morning bend their head
High held in virgin state majestical,
　So meekly cowered those swans in holy dread

---

[1] The current running between Cantire, in Scotland, and the
northern coast of Ireland.
[2] Achill Island, on the coast of Connaught.
[3] The ' Tonsured One,' *i.e.* St. Patrick.

Hearing that promised Tailkenn's blissful name :
For they long since had heard in dream the same.

Then fell a dew of meekness on the proud
    Noting their humble heart ; and drooped her front ;
And sorrow closed around her like a cloud ;
    And thus with other voice than was her wont
To those soft victims of her wrath she cried :
'Woe, woe ! Yet Fate must rule, whate'er betide !

'The deed is done ; yet thus much I concede :
    In you the human heart shall never fail,
Changed though ye be, and masked in feathery weed :
    Your voice shall sweet remain as voice of Gael ;
And all who hear your songs shall sink in trance
And, sleeping, dream some great deliverance.'

She spake, and smote her hands ; and at her word
    Once more the attendants caught the royal steeds
Grazing in peace beside the hornèd herd
    Amid the meadow flowers, and yellow weeds :
And fiercely through the night that dark one drave,
And reached Lough Derg what time above its wave

The sun was rising ; and at set of sun
    Entered once more her father's palace gate :
Seated thereby, his nobles, every one,
    Arose and welcomed her with loving state :

She answered naught, but sternly past them strode
And found her girlhood's bower, and there abode.

But when of Lir King Bove had made demand,
　She answered thus: 'Enough! My Lord is naught;
Nor will he trust his children to thy hand,
　Lest thou should'st slay them.' Long in silent
　　thought
The old man stood, then murmured in low tone,
'I loved those children better than mine own !'

That night in dream King Lir had anguish sore,
　And southward, ere the dawn, rode far away
With many a chief to see his babes once more
　Beside Lough Derg; and lo, at close of day
Nighing to Darvra's lake, the westering sun
In splendour on the advancing horsemen shone.

Straightway from that broad water's central stream
　Was heard a clang of pinions and swift feet—
Unchanged at heart those babes had caught that gleam;
　Instant from far had rushed, their sire to greet
Spangling the flood with silver spray; and ere
That sire had reached the margin they were there.

Then, each and all, clamorous they made lament
　Recounting all their wrong, and all the woe;
And Lir, their tale complete, his garment rent,
　Till then transfixed like marble shape; and lo !

Three times, heart-grieved, that concourse raised their
    cry
Piercing the centre of the low-hung sky.

But Lir knelt down upon the shining sand,
    And cried, ' Though great the might of Druid charms,
Return and feel once more your native land,
    And find once more and fill your father's arms ! '
And they made answer : ' Till the Tailkenn come
We tread not land ! The waters are our home.'

But when Finola saw her father's grief
    She added thus : ' Albeit our days are sad,
The twilight brings our pain in part relief :
    And songs are ours by night that make us glad :
Yea, each that hears our music, though he grieve,
Rejoices more. Abide, for it is eve.'

So Lir, and his, couched on the wave-lipped sod
    All night ; and ever as those songs up swelled
A mist of sleep upon them fell from God,
    And healing Spirits converse with them held.
And Lir was glad all night : but with the morn
Anguish returned ; and thus he cried, forlorn :

' Farewell ! The morn is come ; and I depart :
    Farewell ! Not wholly evil are things ill !
Farewell, Finola ! Yea, but in my heart
    With thee I bide : there liv'st thou changeless still :

O Aodh ! O.Fiacre ! the night is gone :—
Farewell to both ! Farewell, my little Conn

Southward the childless father rode once more,
    And saw at last beyond the forests tall
The great lake and the palace on its shore ;
    And, entering, onward passed from hall to hall
To where King Bove majestic sat and crowned,
High on a terrace, with his magnates round ;

A stately terrace clustered round with towers,
    And jubilant with music's merry din,
Beaten by resonant waves, and bright with flowers :
    There—but apart—she stood that wrought the sin,
Like one that broods on one black thought alone
Seen o'er a world of happy hopes o'erthrown.

The throng made way : onward the wronged one strode
    To Bove, sole-throned, and lifting in his hand
For royal sceptre that Druidic rod
    Which gave him o'er the Spirit-world command ;
Then, pointing to that traitress, false as fair,
That wronged one spake: 'There stands the murderess !
        —there !'

Straight on the King Druidic insight fell ;
    And mirrored in his mind as cloud in lake
His daughter's crime, distinct and visible,
    Before him stood.   He turned to her and spake :

'Thou hear'st the charge : how makest thou reply?
And she : ''The deed is mine ! I wrought it ! I !'

Then spake King Bove with countenance like night :
   'Of all dread shapes that traverse earth or sea,
Or pierce the soil, or urge through heaven their flight,
   Say, which abhorrest thou most?' And answered she :
'The shape of Spirits Accursed that ride the storm :'
And he : 'Be thine henceforth that demon form !'

He spake, and lifted high his Druid Wand :—
   T'ward him perforce she drew : she bowed her head :
Down on that head he dropp'd it ; and beyond
   The glooming lake, with bat-like wings outspread
O'er earth's black verge the shrieking Fury passed ;
Thenceforth to circle earth while earth shall last.

As when, on autumn eve from hill or cape
   That slants into gray wastes of western sea,
The sun long set, some shepherd stares agape
   At cloud that seems through endless space to flee
On raven pinions down the moaning wind,
Thus on that Fury stared they, well-nigh blind.

Then spake the king with hoary head that shook,
   'I loved thy babes : now therefore let us go
Northward, and on their blameless beauty look,
   Though changed, and hear their songs : for this I know

By Druid art, they sing the whole night long,
And heaven and earth are solaced by their song.

Northward ere dawn they rode with a great host ;
   And loosed their steeds by Darvra's mirror clear
What time purpureal evening like a ghost
   Stepped from the blue glen on the glimmering mere :
And camped where stood the ruminating herds
With heads forth leaning t'ward those human birds.

And, ever o'er the wave those swans would come
   To hear man's voice, and tell their tale to each,
Swift as the wind, and whiter than the foam ;
   Yet never mounted they the bowery beach,
And still swerved backward from the beckoning hand,
Revering thus their stepmother's command.

And ever, when the sacred night descended,
   While with those ripples on the sandy bars
The sighing woods and winds low murmurs blended,
   Their music fell upon them from the stars,
And they gave utterance to that gift divine
In silver song or anthem crystalline.

Who heard that strain no more his woes lamented :
   The exiled chief forgat his place of pride :
The prince ill-crowned his ruthless deed repented :
   The childless mother and the widowed bride

Amid their locks tear-wet and loosely straying
Felt once again remembered touches playing.

The words of that high music no one knew ;
 Yet all men felt there lived a meaning there
Immortal, marvellous, searching, strengthening, true,
 The pledge of some great future, strange and fair,
When sin shall lose her might, and cleansing woe
Shall on the Just some starry crown bestow.

Lulled by that strain the prophet king let drop
 In death his Druid-Staff by Darvra's side ;
And there in later years with happy hope
 King Lir, that mystic requiem listening, died :
And there those blissful sufferers bore their wrong
All day in weeping, and all night in song.

Not once 'tis whispered in that ancient story
 They raised their voice God's justice to arraign :
All patient suffering is expiatory :
 Their doom was linked with hope of Erin's gain ;
And, like the Holy Elders famed of old,
Those babes on that high promise kept their hold.

And they saw great towers built, and saw them fall ;
 And saw the little seedling tempest-sown ;
And generations under torch and pall
 Borne forth to narrow graves ere long grass-grown ;

And all these things to them were as a dream,
Or shade that sleeps on some fast hurrying stream.

More numerous daily flocked to that still shore
   Peace-loving spirits : yea, the Gaelic clans
And tribes Dedannan, foemen there no more,
   From the same fountains brimmed their flowing cans,
And washed their kirtles in the same pure rills,
And brought their corn-sheaves to the self-same mills.

Thus, though elsewhere the sons of Erin strove
   From Aileach's coast, and Uladh's marble cliffs,
To where by banks of Lee, and Beara's cove,
   The fishers spread their nets and launched their skiffs,
Round Darvra's shores remained inviolate peace ;
There too the flocks and fields had best increase.

In that long strife the Gael the victory won :
   Tuatha's race, Dedannan, disappeared ;
Yet still the conqueror whispered, sire to son,
   ' Their progeny survives, half scorned, half feared,
The Fairy Host ; and mansions bright they hold
On moonlight hills, and under waters cold.

' To snare the Gael, perpetual spells they weave :
   O'er the wet waste they bid the meteor glide :
They raise illusive cliffs at morn and eve
   On wintry coasts : sea-mantled rocks they hide :

And shipwrecked sailors eye them o'er the waves,
Dark shapes pygmean couchant in sea-caves.

'Some say that, mid the mountains' sunless walls,
　They throng beneath their stony firmament,
An iron-handed race.　At intervals
　Through chasm stream-cloven, and through rocky rent,
The shepherd hears their multitudinous hum
As of far hosts approaching swift yet dumb.

'In those dread vaults, Magian and Alchemist,
　Supreme in every craft of brain and hand,
The mountains' mineral veins they beat and twist ;
　And on red anvils forge them spear and brand
For some predestined battle.　Yea, men say
The island shall be theirs that last great day !'

CANTO THE SECOND.

WHAT time, forth sliding from the Eternal Gates,
   The centuries three on earth had lived and died,
Thus spake Finola to her snowy mates,
   'No more in this soft haven may we bide :
The second Woe succeeds ; that heavier toil
On Alba's waves, the black sea-strait of Moyle.'

Then wept to her in turn the younger three ;
   ' Alas the sharp rocks and the salt sea-foam !
Thou therefore make the lay, ere yet we flee
   From this our exile's cradle, sweet as home ! '
And thus Finóla sang, while, far and near,
The men of Erin wept that strain to hear :

' Farewell, Lough Darvra, with thine isles of bloom !
   Farewell, familiar tribes that grace her shore !
The penance deepens on us, and the doom :
   Farewell !   The voice of man we list no more
Till he, the Tailkenn, comes to sound the knell
Of darkness, and rings out his gladsome bell.'

Thus singing, mid their dirge the sentenced soared
   Heaven-high ; then hanging mute on plumes outspread,
With downcast eye long time that lake explored ;
   And lastly with a great cry northward sped :
Then was it Erin's sons, listening that cry,
Decreed : 'The man who slays a swan shall die.'

Three days against the northern blast on-flying
   To Fate obedient and the Will Divine,
They reached, what time the crimson eve was lying
   On Alba's isles, and ocean's utmost line,
That huge sea-strait whose racing eddies boil
'Twixt Erin and the cloud-girt headland Moyle.[1]

There anguish fell on them : they heard the booming
   Of league-long breakers white, and gazed on waves
Wreck-strewn, themselves entombed, and all-entombing,
   Rolling to labyrinths dim of red-roofed caves ;
And streaming waters broad, as with one will
In cataracts from gray shelves descending still.

There, day by day, the sun more early set ;
   And through the hollows of the high-ridged sea
Which foamed around their rocky cabinet
   The whirlwinds beat them more remorselessly :

---

[1] 'The term *Mael*, Mull (or Moyle, as Moore calls it), does not properly apply to the current itself, but to the *Mael*, or bald headland by which it runs.'—*Professor Eugene O'Curry.*

And winter followed soon : and ofttimes storms
Shrouded for weeks the mountains' frowning forms.

In time all ocean omens they had learned ;
　　And once, as o'er the darkening deep they roved,
Finola, who the advancing woe discerned,
　　Addressed them : ' Little brothers, well beloved,
Though many a storm hath tried us, yet the worst
Comes up this night : now therefore, ere it burst

' Devise we swiftly if, through God's high Will,
　　Billow or blast divides us each from each,
Some refuge-house wherein, when winds are still,
　　To meet once more—low rock or sandy beach :'
And answer thus they made : ' One spot alone
This night can yield us refuge, Carickrone.'

They spake, and sudden thunder shook the world,
　　And blackness wrapped the seas, and lightnings rent :
And each from each abroad those swans were hurled
　　By solid water-scud.　Outworn and spent
At last, that direful tempest over-blown,
Finola scaled their trysting-rock—alone.

But when she found no gentle brother near,
　　And heard the great storm roaring far away,
Anguish of anguish pierced her heart, and fear,
　　And thus she made her moan and sang her lay :

H

' Death-cold they lie along the far sea-tide :
Would that as cold I drifted at their side ! '

Thus as she sang, behold, the sun uprose,
   And smote a swan that on a wave's smooth
     crest
Exhausted lay, like one by pitiless foes
   Trampled, and looking but to death for rest :
He also clomb that rock, though weak and worn,
With bleeding feet and pinions tempest-torn.

Aodh was he !   He couched him by her side ;
   Straight, her right wing, Finola o'er him spread :
Ere long beneath the rock Fiacre she spied,
   Wounded yet more ; yet soon he hid his head
'Neath her left wing, her nestling's wonted place,
And slept content in that beloved embrace.

But still Finola mused with many a tear,
   ' Alas for us, of little Conn bereft ! '
Then Conn came floating by, full blithe of cheer,
   For he, secure within a craggy cleft,
Had slept all night ; and now once more his nest
He made beneath his snowy sister's breast.

And as they slept she sang : ' Among the flowers
   Of old we played where princes quaffed their wine :
But now for flowery fields sea-floods are ours ;
   And now our wine-cup is the bitter brine :

Yet, brothers, fear no ill ; for God will send
At last his Tailkenn, and our woes find end.'

And God, Who of least things has tenderest thought,
   Looked down on them benignly from on high,
And bade that bitter brine to enter not
   Their scars, unhealed as yet, lest they should die :
And nearer sent their choicest food full oft,
And clothed their wings with plumage fine and soft.

And ever as the spring advanced, the sea
   Put on a kindlier aspect.   Cliffs deep-scarred
To milder airs gave welcome festively
   Upon their iron breasts and foreheads hard,
And, while about their feet the ripples played,
Cast o'er the glaring deep a friendlier shade.

And when at last the full midsummer panted
   Upon the austere main, and high-peaked isles,
And hills that, like some elfin land enchanted,
   Now charmed, now mocked the eye with phantom
      smiles,
More far round Alba's shores the swans made way
To Islay's beach, and cloud-loved Colonsay.

The growths beside their native lake oft noted
   In that sublimer clime no more they missed ;
Jewels, not flowers they found where'er they floated,
   Emerald and sapphire, opal, amethyst,

Far-kenned through watery depths or magic air,
Or trails of broken rainbows, here and there.

Round Erin's northern coasts they drifted on
   From Rathlin isle to Fanad's beetling crest,
And where, in frowning sunset steeped, forth shone
   The 'Bloody Foreland,' gazing t'ward the west ;
Yet still with duteous hearts to Moyle returned—
To love their place of penance they had learned.

One time it chanced that, onward as they drifted
   Where Banna's current joins that stormy sea,
A princely company with banners lifted
   Rode past on snow-white steeds and sang for glee :
At once they knew those horsemen, form and face,
Their native stock—Tuatha's ancient race !

T'ward them they sped : their sorrows they recounted :
   The warriors could not aid them, and rode by :
Then higher than of old their anguish mounted ;
   And farther rang through heaven their piteous cry ;
And when it ceased, this lay Finola sang
While all the echoing rocks and caverns rang :

'Whilome in purple clad we sat elate :
   The warriors watched us at their nut-brown mead :
But now we roam the waters desolate,
   Or breast the languid beds of waving weed :

Our food was then fine bread ; our drink was wine :
This day on sea-plants sour we peak and pine.

'Whilome our four small cots of pearl and gold
    Lay, side by side, before our father's bed,
And silken foldings kept us from the cold :
    But now on restless waves our couch is spread ;
And now our bed-clothes are the white sea-foam :
And now by night the sea-rock is our home.'

Not less from them such sorrows swiftly passed
    Since evermore one thought their bosoms filled—
That father's home. That haunt, in memory glassed.
    Childhood perpetual o'er their lives distilled :
And, coast what shore they might, green vale and plain
Bred whiter flocks, men said, more golden grain.

The years ran on : the centuries three went by :
    Finola sang : 'The second Woe is ended ! '
Obedient then, once more they soared on high ;
    Next morn on Erin's western coast descended,
While sunrise flashed from misty isles far seen,
Now gold, now flecked with streaks of luminous green.

And there for many a winter they abode,
    Harbouring in precincts of the setting sun ;
And mourned by day, yet sang at night their ode
    As though in praise of some great victory won :

Some conqueror more than man ; some heavenly crown
Slowly o'er all creation settling down.

There once—what time a great sun in decline
   Had changed to gold the green back of a wave
That showered a pasture fair with diamond brine,
   Then sank, anon uprising from its grave
Went shouldering onward, higher and more high,
And hid far lands, and half eclipsed the sky—

There once a shepherd, Aibhric, high of race,
   Marked them far off, and marking them so loved
That to the ocean's verge he rushed apace
   With hands outspread. Shoreward the creatures
      moved ;
And when he heard them speak with human tongue
That love he felt grew tenderer and more strong.

Day after day they told that youth their tale :
   Wide-eyed he stood, and inly drank their words ;
And later, harping still in wood and vale,
   He fitted oft their sorrow to his chords ;
And thus to him in part men owe the lore [1]
Of all those patient sufferers bare of yore.

[1] 'They met a young man of good family whose name was
Aibhric, and his attention was often attracted to the birds, and their
singing was sweet to him, so that he came to love them greatly, and
that they loved him ; and it was this young man that afterwards
arranged in order and narrated all their adventures.'—*The Fate of
the Children of Lir*, prose version by Professor O'Curry.

For bard he was ; and still the bard-like nature
   Hath reverence, as for virtue, so for woe,
And ever finds in trials of the creature
   The great Creator's purpose here below
To lift by lowering, and through anguish strange
To fit for thrones exempt from chance or change.

There first the Four had met that sympathy
   Yearned for so long : and yet, that treasure found,
So much the more ere long calamity
   Tasked them, thus strengthened ; tasked and closed
      them round,
And higher yet fierce winds and watery shocks
Dashed them thenceforth upon the pitiless rocks.

At last from heaven's dark vault a night there fell
   The direst they had known. The high-heaped
      seas
Vanquished by frost, beneath her iron spell
   Abased their haughty crests by slow degrees :
The swans were frozen upon that ice-plain frore ;
Yet still Finola sang, as oft before,

' Beneath my right wing, Aodh, make thy rest !
   Beneath my left, Fiacre ! My little Conn,
Find thou a warmer shelter 'neath my breast,
   As thou art wont : thou art my little son !
Thou God that all things mad'st, and lovest all,
Subdue things great ! Protect the weak, the small ! '

But evermore the younger three made moan ;
   And still their moans more loud and louder grew ;
And still Finola o'er that sea of stone
   For their sake fragments of wild wailings threw ;
And ever as she sang, the on-driving snow
Choked the sweet strain ; yet still she warbled low.

Then, louder when she heard those others grieve,
   And found that song might now no more avail,
She said : ' Believe, O brothers young, believe
   In that great God, whose help can never fail !
Have faith in God, since God can ne'er deceive !'
And lo, those weepers answered : 'We believe !'

So thus those babes, in God's predestined hour,
   Through help of Him, the Lord of Life and Death,
Inly fulfilled with light and prophet power,
   Believed ; and perfect made their Act of Faith ;
And thenceforth all things, both in shade and shine,
To them came softly and with touch benign.

First, from the southern stars there came a breeze
   On-wafting happy mist of moonlit rain ;
And when the sun ascended o'er the seas
   The ice was vanquished ; and the watery plain
And every cloud with rapture thrilled and stirred :
And lo, at noon the cuckoo's voice was heard !

And since with that rough ice their feet were sore
 God for their sake a breeze from Eden sent
That gently raised them from the ocean's floor
 And in its bosom, as an ambient tent,
Held them, suspense : and with a dew of balm
God, while they slept, made air and ocean calm.

Likewise a beam auroral forth he sped
 That flushed that tent aerial like a rose
Each morn, and roseate odours o'er it shed
 The long day through.   And still, at evening's close,
They dreamed of those rich bowers and alleys green
Wherein with Lir their childish sports had been.

And thrice they dreamed that in the morning gray
 They gathered there red roses drenched with dew :
But lo ! a serpent 'neath the roses lay :
 Then came the Tailkenn, and that serpent slew ;
And round the Tailkenn's tonsured head was light
That made that morning more than noonday bright.

Thus wrapt, thus kindled, in sublimer mood
 Heaven-high they soared, and flung abroad their strain
O'er-sailing huge Croagh-Patrick swathed in wood,
 Or Acaill, warder of the western main,
Or Arran Isle, that time heroic haunt,
Since Enda's day Religion's saintlier vaunt.

And many a time they floated farther south
   Where milder airs endear sea-margins bleak,
To that dim Head far seen o'er Shenan's mouth,
   Or Smerwick's ill-famed cliff and winding creek,
Or where on Brandon sleeps Milesius' son
With all his shipwrecked warriors round him—Donn.

The centuries passed : her loud, exultant lay
   Finola sang, their time of penance done,
And ended : ' Lo, to us it seems a day ;
   Not less the dread nine hundred years are run !
Now, brothers, homeward be our flight !'   And they
Chanted triumphant : 'Home, to Finnahá !'

Up from the sea they rose in widening gyre,
   And hung suspended mid the ethereal blue,
And saw, far-flashing in the sunset's fire,
   A wood-girt lake whose splendour well they knew ;
And flew all night ; and reached at dawn its shore—
Ah, then rang out that wail ne'er heard before !

There where the towers of Lir of old had stood
   Lay now the stony heap and rain-washed rath ;
And through the ruin-mantling alder-wood
   The forest beast had stamped in mire his path ;
And desolate were their mother's happy bowers,
So fair of old with fountains and with flowers !

More closely drew the orphans, each to each :—
　"Twas then Finola raised her dirge on high,
As nearer yet they drifted to the beach
　In hope one fragment of past days to spy ;
' Upon our father's house hath fallen a change ;
And as a dead man's face this place is strange !

' No more the hound and horse ; no more the horn !
　No more the warriors winding down the glen !
Behold, the place of pleasaunce is forlorn,
　And emptied of fair women and brave men ;
The wine-cup now is dry ; the music fled :
Now know we that our father, Lir, is dead ! '

She sang, and ceased, though long the feathered throat
　Panted with passion of the unuttered song :
At last she spake with voice that seemed remote
　Like echoed voice of one the tombs among :
' Depart we hence !　Better the exile's pain ! '
And they : ' Return we to rough waves again ! '

Yet still along that silver mere they lingered
　Oaring their weeping way by lawn and cape,
Till evening, purple-stoled and dewy-fingered,
　O'er heaven's sweet face had woven its veil of crape ;
And tenderer came from darkening wood and wild
The voice far off of woman or of child.

And when, far travelling through the fields of ether,
   The stars successive filled their thrones of light,
Still to that heaven the glimmering lake beneath her
   Gave meet response, with music answering light ;
For still, wherever sailed that mystic four,
With minstrelsy divine that lake ran o'er.

But when the rising sun made visible
   The night-mist hovering long o'er banks of reed
They cast their broad wings on a gathering swell
   Of wind that, late from eastern sea-caves freed,
Waved all the island's oakwoods t'ward the West ;
And seaward swooped at eve, and there found rest.

And since they knew their penance now was over,
   Penance that tasks true hearts to purify,
Happier were they than e'er was mortal lover,
   Happy as Spirits cleansed that, near the sky,
Feel, mid that shadowy realm expiatory,
Warm on their lids the unseen yet nearing glory.

Thenceforth they roamed no more, at Inisglaire
   Their change awaiting.   In its blissful prime
That island was, men say, as Eden fair,
   The swan-soft nurseling of a changeful clime,
With amaranth-lighted glades, and tremulous sheen
Of trees full-flowered on earth no longer seen.

Not then the waves with that still site contended ;
  On its warm sandhills pansies always bloomed ;
And ever with the inspiring sea-wind blended
  The breath of gardens violet-perfumed ;
And daisies whitened lawn and dell, and spread
At sunset o'er green hills their under-red,

Faint as that blush which lights some matron's cheek
  Tenderly pleased by gentle praise deserved—
That island's winding coast from creek to creek
  Like curves of shells with dream-like beauty swerved :
And midmost spread a lake ; from mortal eyes
Vanished this day like man's lost paradise.

Around that lake with oldest oakwoods shaded
  Were all things that to eye are witching most,
Green slopes, dew drenched, and gray rocks ivy-braided;
  Yet speechless was the region as a ghost :
No whisper shook those woods ; no tendril stirred ;
Nor e'er beside the cave was ripple heard.

A home for Spirits, not home for man, it seemed ;
  Or Limbo meet for body-waiting Souls—
Of such in Pagan times the poets dreamed—
  That stillness which invests the unmoving poles
Above it brooded.   In its circuit wide
A second Darvra lived—but glorified.

Upon its breast perpetual light there lay,
 Undazzling beam, and uncreated light ;
For lake and wood the sunshine drank all day,
 And breathed it softly forth to cheer the night,
A silver twilight, pure from cloud or taint,
Like aureole round the forehead of a saint.

There dwelt those Swans; there louder anthems chanted :
 There first they sang by day—rapt song and hymn,
Till all those birds the western coasts that haunted
 Came flying far o'er ocean's purple rim,
Scorning thenceforth wild cliff and beds of foam ;
And made, then first, that sacred isle their home.

So passed three years. When dawned the third May morn
 The Four, while slowly rose the kindling mist
Showing the first white on the earliest thorn,
 Heard music o'er the waters. List, O list !
'Twas sweet as theirs—more sweet—yet terrible
At first ; and sudden trembling on them fell.

A second time it sounded. Terror died,
 And rapture came instead, and mystic mirth
They knew not whence : and thus Finola cried :
 ' Brothers ! the Tailkenn treads our Erin's earth ! '
And as the lifted mist gave view more large
They saw a blue bay with a fair green marge.

On that green marge there rose an Altar-stone :
  Before it, robed in white, with tonsured head,
Stood up the kingly Tailkenn all alone :
  Not far behind, in reverence, not in dread,
With low bent brows a princely senate knelt,
Girding that altar as with golden belt.

Marvelling, as on they sailed that Rite they saw :
  But, when a third time pealed that Tailkenn's bell,
They too their halleluias, though with awe,
  Blended with his.   The Ill Spirits heard their knell,
And shrieking fled to penal dungeons drear ;
And straight, since now those blissful Four drew near,

Saint Patrick stretched above the wave his hand
  And thus he spake—and wind and wave were stilled—
'Children of Lir, re-tread your native land,
  For now your long sea-penance is fulfilled ! '
Then lo ! Finola raised the funeral cry :
' We tread our native land that we may die ! '

And thus she made the lay, and thus she sang :
  'Baptize us, priest, while living yet we be ! '
And louder soon her dirge-like anthem rang :
  ' Lo, thus the Children's burial I decree :
Make fair our grave where land and ocean meet ;
And t'ward thy holy Altar place our feet.

' Upon my left, Fiacre ; upon my right
    Let Aodh sleep ; for such their place of rest,
Secured to each by usage and by right :
    And lay my little Conn upon my breast :
Then on a low sand pillow raise my head,
That I may see his face though I be dead.'

She spake ; and on the sands they stept—the Four—
    Then lo, from heaven there came a miracle :
Soon as they left the wave, and trod the shore
    The weight of bygone centuries on them fell :
To human forms they changed, yet human none ;—
Dread, shapeless weights of wrinkles and of bone.

A moment prone the wildered creatures lay ;
    Then slowly up that breadth of tawny sand,
Like wounded beast that can but crawl, made way
    With knee convulsed, and closed and clutching hand,
Nine-centuried forms, still breathing mortal breath,
Though shrouded in the cerements pale of death.

That concourse on them gazed with many a tear ;
    Yet no man uttered speech or motion made,
Till now the Four had reached that altar-bier,
    Their ghastly pilgrimage's goal, and laid
Before its base their bodies, one by one,
And faces glistening in the rising sun.

There lying, loud they raised the self-same cry,
    As Patrick o'er them signed the conquering Sign,
' Baptize us, holy Tailkenn, for we die ! '
    The saint baptized them in the Name Divine,
And, swift as thought, their happy spirits at last
To God's high feast and singing angels passed.

Now hear the latest wonder. While, low-bowed,
    That concourse gazed upon the reverend dead
Behold, like changeful shapes in evening cloud,
    Vanished those time-worn bodies ; and, instead,
Inwoven lay four children, white and young
With silver-lidded eyes and lashes long.

Finola lay, once more an eight years' child :
    Upon her right hand Aodh took his rest.
Upon her left Fiacre ;—in death he smiled :
    Her little Conn was cradled on her breast :
And all their saintly raiment shone as bright
As sea-foam sparkling on a moonlit night ;

Or as their snowy night-clothes shone of old!
    When now the night was past, and Lir. their sire,
Upraised them from the warm cot's silken fold.
    And bade them watch the sun's ascending fire,
And watched himself its beam, now here now there,
Flashed from white foot, blue eyes, or golden hair.

The men who saw that deathbed did not weep,
  But gazed till sunset upon each fair face ;
And then with funeral psalm, and anthems deep,
  Interred them at that sacred altar's base,
And graved their names in Ogham characters
On one white tomb ; and, close beneath them, Lir's.

Those Babes were Erin's Holy Innocents,
  And first-fruits of the land to Christ their Lord,
Though born within the unbelievers' tents :
  Figured in them the Gael his God adored,
That later-coming, holier Gael, who won
Through Faith the birthright, though the younger son

THE

FORAY OF QUEEN MEAVE

OR

'THE TAIN BO CUAILGNÉ'

FIVE FRAGMENTS OF AN ANCIENT IRISH EPIC

TO

SIR SAMUEL FERGUSON

THIS POEM IS DEDICATED,

IN   TOKEN   OF   GRATITUDE

FOR 'CONGAL,' AND FOR MANY POEMS BESIDE,

THAT ILLUSTRATE ARIGHT

THE LEGENDS OF ANCIENT IRELAND.

PROLOGUE.

Senchan, the king of bards, when centuries six
Had flowered and faded since the Birth Divine,
Summoned in synod all the island bards,
Demanding ; ' Is there who can yet recite
That first of Erin's songs, " The Tain " ? '   Not one
Could sing it, save in fragments.   Then arose
Marbhan, and spake ; ' Send prayer to Erin's Saints
That, bowed o'er Fergus' grave, they lift their hands
For Erin at her need.'   Five Saints obeyed
And o'er that venerable spot three days
Fasting made prayer while knelt the bards around.
Then on the third day as the sun uprose
Behold ! a purple mist engirt that grave ;
And from it, fair as rainbow backed by cloud,
Shone out a kingly Phantom robed in green,
With red-brown locks, close clustered, drenched in dew,
And golden crown, and golden-hilted sword ;—
His hand was on it.   They who saw that Shape
Well knew him, Fergus Roy, the Exile-King.

Gracious as in the old days, that king rehearsed
The Tale so long desired, though many an age,
And that grey empire of departed Souls,
Had quelled at last the strong ones of that strain,
Record half jest, half earnest.   Marbhan spoke
Once more ; ' Lest Erin lose again this Tale
Through fraud of demons or all-wasting time,
Amid yon Saints elect some scribe, their best,
And pray that scribe to write it.'   Straight, with help
It may be, of the bards, Saint Kiaran wrote
The Heroic Song on parchment fine, the skin
Of one he loved, his ' little heifer grey '
That gave the book its name.   Six centuries passed ;
Then in Saint Kiaran's House at Clonmacnoise
That book was found, and on it ; ' Reader, here
Are histories old with later fables blent,
Fancies full fair with idle Pagan vaunts :
Now therefore, since old things have in them worth
And teach by what they hold and what they lack
Whoso shall read this book, and know to choose
'Twixt Good and Ill, my blessing on him rest ! '

FRAGMENT I.

THE CAUSE OF THE GREAT WAR.

ARGUMENT.

MEAVE, Queen of Connacht,[1] and Ailill her husband, waking one morning fall into a disputation, each claiming to be the worthier of the two, and the wealthier. Their lords decide that the king and queen are great and happy alike in all things save one only, namely, that Ailill possesses the far-famed white Bull, Fionbannah. Meave hearing that Conor Conchobar, King of Uladh,[2] boasts a black Bull mightier yet, is fain to purchase it, but cannot prevail so far. She therefore declares war against Uladh. There meets her Fayth-leen the Witch, who prophesies calamity, but promises that in aid of Meave she will breathe over the realm of Uladh a spirit of im-becility. This she does ; yet Cuchullain, unaided, afflicts the whole army of Meave by exploits which to him are but sports. Fergus, the exiled King of Uladh, narrates to Meave the high deeds of Cuchullain wrought in his childhood.

IN Cruachan, old Connacht's palace pile,
Dwelt Meave, the queen, haughtiest of woman's kind,
A warrioress untamed that made her will
The measure of the world. The all-conquering years
Conquered not her : the strength of endless prime

---

[1] Now Connaught.   [2] Now Ulster.

Lived in her royal tread and breast and eye
A life immortal.   Queenly was her brow ;
Fulgent her eye ; her countenance beauteous, save
When wrath o'er-flamed its beauty.   With her dwelt
Ailill her husband, trivial man and quaint,
And early old.   He had not chosen her :
She chose a consort who should rule her not,
And tossed him to her throne.   In youth her lord
Was Conor Conchobar, great Uladh's King :
She had not found him docile to her will,
And to her sire returned.   The August morn
Had trailed already on the stony floor
Its fiery beam when, laughing, Ailill woke :
He woke, awakened by a sound that shook
The forest dews to earth, Fionbannah's roar,
That snow-white Bull, the wonder of the age,
Who, born amid the lowlands of the queen,
Yet, grown to strength, o'er-leaped her bound and roamed
Thenceforth the leaner pastures of the king,
For this cause, that his spirit scorned to live
In female vassalage.
                    That tale recalling
King Ailill laughed : his laughter roused the queen :
She woke in wrath : to assuage her Ailill spake ;
' Happy and blest that dame whose lord is sage !
Thy fortunes, wife of mine, began that day

I called thee spouse !'· To him the queen, 'My sire
Was Erin's Ard-Righ ! [1] Daughters six had he :
I, Meave, of these was fairest and most famed !
This Cruachan was mine before we met ;
And all the Island's princes sued my hand.
I spurned their offers ! three things I required—
A warrior proved, since great at arms am I ;
A liberal hand, since lavish I of gifts ;
A man not jealous, since, in love as war,
There where I willed I ever cast mine eyes.
These merits three were yours : I beckoned to you :
Dowered you with ingots thicker than your wrist ;
Made you a king, or kingling.   What of that ?
I might have chosen a better !   Yea, I count
My greatness more than yours !'

                              With treble shrill
Ailill replied ; ' What words are these, my queen ?
My father was a king ; my brothers kings !
My hoards are higher heaped than yours ; my meads
More deep, more rich !'
                       Then loudly stormed the queen :—
In rushed her lords, and stood, a senate grave,
Circling the couch : and while, each answering each,
Ailill and Meave set forth in order due
The treasures either boasted, kine, or sheep,

[1] Chief King.

Rich cornfield, jewel'd robe, or gem-wrought car,
Careful they weighed the lists in equal scale
And 'twixt them found in value difference none.
Doubtful they stood.   Anon rolled forth once more
Fionbannah's roar ; and, leaping from his bed
King Ailill shouted ; ' Mine, not thine, that Bull !
Through him my treasure passes thine, my queen !
My worth exceeds thy worth ! '   At once forth stepped
Mac Roth, old Connacht's herald, with this word :
' Great queen, the King of Uladh boasts a Bull
Lordlier than ours, a broader bulk, and black,
Black as the raven's wing !   In Daré's charge
That marvel bides, the Donn Cuailgné named
Because his lowings shake Cuailgné's shore,
The southern bound of Uladh.   Privilege
He hath that neither witch nor demon tempt
That precinct where he harbours.'   Meave exclaimed,
' Fly hence, Mac Roth !   Take with thee golden store,
Rich garments, chariots gemmed : bid Daré choose ;
But bring me back that Bull ! '

                  Three days had passed :
Then by the tower of Daré stood Mac Roth
And blew his horn ; and Daré's sons with speed
Flung the gate wide.   The herald entered in
And spake his message.   Proudly Daré mused,
' Great Meave my friendship sues ; ' and made a feast,

And, when the wine had warmed him spake ; 'Mac
    Roth !
Cuailgné's Donn is Conor's Bull, not mine :
Yet, though the king should hurl me outcast forth,
To Meave that Bull shall go and bide a year.
Tell her-the Donn is manlike in his mind,
And not like Bulls.   Long summer eves he stands,
Or paces stately up the mead and down
Eyeing the racing youths, or glad at heart
Listening the music.'   Thus he pledged his faith.
But Daré's sons at midnight, each to each,
Whispered ; 'the king will chase us from the realm !
He hates Queen Meave, and well he loves the Donn ;'
And stood next morn beside their sire, and spake,
'Mac Roth is gone a hunting : ere he went
He sware that you had yielded him the Donn
Fearing his sword.'   Then Daré's heart was changed,
And loud by all his swearing Gods he sware
'Cuailgné's Donn shall ne'er consort with Meave,
Nor with her kine :' and on his gate he set
The castle's Fool waiting Mac Roth's return,
And charged him with this greeting ; 'Back to Meave !
Thy queen she is, not Uladh's !   Bid her know
Our Donn and we revere Fionbannah's choice,
Her Bull, that leaped her gate and swam her flood,
Spurning the female rule !'

Then turned Mac Roth
His car ; and sideway shook one hand irate ;
And lashed the steeds, and reached great Cruachan,
And, instant upon all who heard his tale
Like lightning fell the battle rage.   The queen,
Sent forth her heralds, east, and west, and south,
Summoning her great allies.   Erin, that day
Save Uladh only, stood conjoined with Meave,
Great kings, and warriors named from chiefs of old
Sons of Milesius ; for King Conor's craft
And that proud onset of the Red-Branch Knights
Year after year had galled their hearts.   'Twas come !
The day of vengeance !   In their might they rose
From Eyrus' vales to utmost Cahirnane,
From Oileen Arda on to Borda Lu,
And where the loud wave breaks on Beara's isle ;
And by the hallowed banks of Darvra's lake
Where, changed to swans, the Children Four of Lir,
Dowerless on earth, their home the homeless waves,
Darkling yet gladdening gloomier hearts with light,
And sad yet solaced through one conquering hope,
By song had vanquished sorrow.   From the West,
Came Inachall, and Adarc.   Eiderkool
Marched, ever shrilling songs and shaking spears :
And, mightier far, with never slumbering hearts
And eyes that stared through long desire of home

Uladh's three thousand exiles, driven far forth
When Conor Conchobar, trampling his pledge,
Slaughtered the sons of Usnach.   At their head
Rode Fergus, Uladh's King ere traitor yet
Had filched its royal crown ; and by his side,
Faithful in exile, Cormac Conlinglas,
King Conor's bravest son.   That host the queen
To Ai led, where Ai's four great plains
Shine in the rising and the setting sun,
Gold-green, with all their flag-flowers, meres, and
        streams :
There planted she her camp ; thence ever rang
Neighing of horse, and tempest song of bard,
And graver voice of prophet and of seer
Who ceased not, day or night, for fifteen days
From warnings to the people, ' Be ye one ; '—
Yet one the people were not.
                Meave the while,
Resting upon those great and growing hosts
Her widening eyes, rejoiced within, and clutched
The sceptre-staff with closer grasp, and heaved
Higher her solid, broad, imperial breast,
Amorous of battle nigh at hand.   Yet oft,
Listening those bickerings in her camp she frowned :
For still the chieftains strove ; and one, a king
Briarind, had tongue so sharp, where'er he moved

A guard was round him set lest spleen of his
Should set the monarchs ravening each on each.
'The hand of Fergus,' mused she, 'that alone
Might solder yonder mass.   Men note in him
His front, his voice, his stature, and his step,
The one time King of Uladh.   Held he rule—
He shall not for my will endures it not !
He props my war because, long years our guest,
His honour needs not less ; with us he marches
Athirst for vengeance and his native land,
Yet scoffs our cause, and sent, spurning surprise,
To Uladh challenge loud.'   Again she mused,
' A man love-worthy if he loved again !—
At best 'twould be to him a moment's sport !
The battle and the stag-hunt, these alone,
He counts a prince's pastimes ! '   Sudden from heaven
Eclipse there fell on Ai's spacious plains,
And shadow black ; these noting, Meave revolved
That dread Red Branch in act and counsel one ;
And, brooding thus, with inner eye she saw
No longer men but skeletons of men
Innumerable in intertangled mass
Burthening the fields far spread.   Aloud she cried,
' On to Moytura where the prophet dwells ; '
And straight her charioteer the horses smote
And tamed them with the reins : and lo ! what time

The noontide sun with keenest splendour blazed,
Right opposite upon the chariot's beam
There sat a wondrous woman phantom-faced
Singing and weaving.   Shapely was that head
Bent o'er her web, while back the sun-like hair
Streamed on the wind.   One hand upreared a sword :
Seven chains fell from it.   Sea-blue were her eyes,
And berry-red her scornful lip ; her cheek
White as the snow-drift of a single night ;
Her voice like harp-strings when the harper's hand
Half drowns their pathos.   Close as bark to tree
The azure robe clung to that virgin form
Sinewy and long, and reached the shining feet.
　　Then spake the queen ; 'What see'st thou in that
　　　web ? '
And she, ' I see a kingdom's destinies ;
And they are like a countenance dashed with blood :
Faythleen am I, the Witch.'   To her the queen ;
' I bid thee say what see'st thou in my host,
Faythleen, the Witch ! '   And Faythleen answered slow,
' The hue of blood : sunset on sunset charged.'
Then fixed that Wild One on the North her eyes,
And Meave made answer ; ' In those eyes I see
The fates they see ; great Uladh's realm full-armed,
And all that Red Branch Order as one man.'
Faythleen replied ; 'One man alone I see ;

One man, yet mightier than a realm in arms !
That Watch-Hound watching still by Uladh's gate
Is mightier thrice than Uladh : on his brow
Spring-tide sits throned ; yet ruin loads his hand.
If e'er Cuchullain rides in Uladh's van
Flee to thy hills and isles ! ' Meave bit her lip :
But wildly sang the Witch ; ' Faythleen am I,
Thy People's patron mid the Powers unseen :
Beware that youth invisible for speed,
Who hears that whisper none beside can hear,
Sees what none other sees ; before whose eye
The wild beast cowers, subdued ! Beware that youth
Slender as maid, whose stature in the fight
Rises gigantic. Gamesome he and mild ;
To woman reverent and the hoary hair ;
Nor alms he stints nor incense to the Gods ;
But when from heaven the anger on him breaks
Pity he knows for none. No pact with him !
Return with speed and march to-morrow morn :
The clan of Cailitin shall yield thee aid,
That magic clan which fights with poisoned darts.
To Uladh I, above her realm to spread
Mantle of darkness, and a mind that errs,
And powerlessness, and shame.'

                  Due north she sped,
Far fleeting, wind-upborne ! 'twixt hill and cloud,

To Uladh's cliffs, and thence with prone descent
Sank to the myriad-murmuring sea wine-dark,
And whispered to the Genii of the deep,
Her sisters :—then from ocean's breast there rose
A mist, no larger than a dead man's shroud,
That, slowly widening, spread o'er Uladh's realm
Mantle of darkness, and an erring mind,
And powerlessness, and shame.

       The queen returned,
And reached her host what time the sunset glare
With omnipresent splendour girt it round,
Concourse immortalised. Thereon she gazed
High standing in her chariot, spear in hand :
Her too that army saw, and raised the shout.
But Fergus, as she passed him spake : 'not yet
Know'st thou my Uladh, nor the Red Branch Knights :
And one man is there mightier thrice than they.'

  Meantime within Murthemné's land its lord
Cuchullain, musing like a listening hound,
For many a rumour filled that time the air,
Sat in remote Dûn Dalgan [1] all alone,
Chief city of his realm. On Uladh's verge
Southward that lesser realm dependent lay
Girt by a racing river. Silent long
He watched : at last he heard a sound like wind

---

[1] Now Dundalk.

K

In woods remote ; and earthward bowed his head ;
And said ; 'that sound is distant thirty leagues,
And huge that host ;' then bade prepare his car,
And southward sped, counsel to hold as wont
With Faythleen nigh to Tara.

               Eve grew dim
When lo ! a chariot from the woods emerged
In swift pursuit : an old man urged the steeds,
A grey old man that chattered evermore
With blinking eyes that ceased not from amaze.
That sight displeased Cuchullain : ne'ertheless
He stayed his course ; and Saltain soon drew nigh,
Clamouring, ' O son—and when was son like thee—
Forsake not thou thy father !   In old time,
Then when some God had laid on me his hand,
Dectara, my wife, immured me in my house,
Year after year, and weighed the lessening dole :
But thou, to manhood grown, though even to her
Reverent, didst pluck her from that place usurped,
Lifting thy poor old father.'   At that word
Cuchullain left his car, and kissed his sire,
And soothed his wandering wits with meat and wine ;
· And spake dissembling ; ' lo, these mantles warm !
Prescient, for thee I stored them !   Night is near ;
Lie down and rest.'   Thus speaking, with both hands
Deftly he spread them wide ; and Saltain slept :

Then, tethering first the horses of his sire,
Lastly his own, upon the chill, wet grass
He likewise lay, and slept not.   ·
                              On, at dawn
They drave ; but Faythleen, witch perverse of will,
That oft´through spleenful change her purpose slew,
Had broken tryst ; and northward they returned.
That day Cuchullain clomb a rock tree-girt
And kenned beyond the forest's roof a host
Innumerable, the standards of Queen Meave,
And Fergus, and the great confederate kings.
The warrior eyed them long with bitter smile ;
Few words he spake : ' At fifty thousand men
I count them.'   To his father then he turned :
· Haste to Emania !   Bid the Red Branch Knights
'.ttend me in Murthemné.   I till then
Hang on the invaders' flank, a fiery scourge.'
      Saltain made answer : ' Be it ! northward I ;
But Dectara, thy mother, and my wife,
Till thou art by my side I will not see ;
For dreadful are her eyes as death or fate ;
And many deem her mad.'
                              He spake, and drave
Northward ; nor ceased from chatterings all day long,
Since, like a Poplar, vocal was the man
Not less than visible.   Meantime his son

Took counsel in his heart, and made resolve
To skirt, in homeward course, that eastern sea,
The woods primeval 'twixt him and the foe,
Still sallying night and day through alley and glade
And taming thus their pride.

       Three days went by :
Then stood Cuchullain where great wood-ways met ;
And lo ! betwixt four yews a warrior's grave,
The pillar-stone above it !   O'er that stone
In mirthful mood he twined an osier wreath,
Cyphering thereon his name in Ogham signs :
For thus he said ; 'On no man unawares
Fall I, but warned.'   The hostile host approached,
And, halting stood in wonder at that wreath ;
Yet none could spell the Ogham.   Last drew nigh
Fergus, and read it : on him fell that hour
Memories full dear, and loud he sang and long ;
He sang a warrior's praise : yet named him not ;
He sang ; 'From name of man to name of beast
A warrior changed : then mightiest grew of men !'
And, as he sang, the cheek of Meave grew red.

  Next morn Neara's sons outsped the rest
Car-borne with brandished spears ; and, ere the dew
Was lifted, came to where Cuchullain sat
Beneath an oak, sporting with black-birds twain
That followed him for aye.   Toward the youths

He waved his hand ; ' Away, for ye are young ! '
In answer forth they flung their spears : he caught them,
And snapt them on his knee ; next, swift as fire,
Sprang on the twain, and slew them with his sword,
One blow :—anon he loosed their horses' bits,
And they, with madness winged, rejoined the host,
Bearing those headless bulks.   Forth looked the queen :
Beheld ; and, trembling, cried ; ' It might have been
Orloff, my son ! '
     That eve, at banquet ranged
The warriors questioned Fergus ; ' Who is best
Among the Uladh chiefs ? '   Ere answer came
King Conor's son self-exiled, Conlinglas,
Upleaping cried, ' Cuchullain is his name !
Cuchullain !   From his childhood man was he !
On Eman Macha [1] ever was his thought,
Its walls, its bulwarks, and its Red Branch Knights,
The wonder of the world.'   Then told the prince
How, when his mother mocked his zeal, that child
Fared forth alone, with wooden sword and shield,
And fife, and silver ball ; and how he hurled
His little spears before him as he ran,
And caught them ere they fell ; and how, arrived,
He spurned great Eman's gates, and scaled its wall,
And lighted in the pleasaunce of the king,

    [1] Armagh.

His mother's brother, Conor Conchobar ;
And how the noble youths of all that land
There trained in warlike arts, had on him dashed
With insult and with blows : and how the child
This way and that had hurled them, while the king
Who sat that hour with Fergus, playing chess,
Gazed from his turret wondering.

                    Next he told
How to that child, Setanta first, there fell
Cuchullain's nobler name.   'To Eman near
There dwelt an armourer, Cullain was his name,
That earliest rose, and latest with his forge
Reddened the night : mail-clad in might of his
The Red Branch Knights forth rode ; the bard, the chief
Claimed him for friend.   One day, when Conor's self
Partook his feast, the armourer held discourse ;
" The Gods have made my house a house of fame :
The craftsmen grin and grudge because I prosper :
The forest bandits hunger for my goods,
Yea, and would eat mine anvil if they might—
Trow ye what saves me, Sirs ?   A Hound is mine,
Each eve I loose him, lion-like, and fell ;
The blood of many a rogue is on his mouth :
The bravest, if they hear him bay far off,
Flee like a deer ! "   Setanta's shout rang loud
That moment at the gate, and, with it blent,

The baying of that hound ! "The boy is dead,"
King Conor cried in horror. Forth they rushed—
There stood he, bright and calm, his rigid hands
Clasping the dead hound's throat ! They wept for joy :
The armourer wept for grief. "My friend is dead !
My friend that kept my house and me at peace :
My friend that loved his lord !" Setanta heard
Then first that cry forth issuing from the heart
Of him whose labour wins his children's bread ;
That cry he honours yet. Red-cheeked he spake ;
"Cullain ! unwittingly I did thee wrong !
I make amends. I, child of kings, henceforth
Abide, thy watch-hound, warder of thy house."
Thenceforth the 'Hound of Cullain'[1] was his name,
And Cullain's house well warded.'

                             Stern of brow
The queen arose : 'Enough of fables, lords !
Drink to the victory ! Ere yon moon is dead
We knock at gates of Eman.' High she held
The crimson goblet. Instant, felt ere heard,
Vibration strange troubled the moonlit air ;
A long-drawn hiss o'er-ran it : then a cry,
Death-cry of warrior wounded to the death.
They rose : they gazed around : upon a rock
Cuchullain stood. The warrior said in heart,

        [1] *Cu* in Irish means hound.

' I will not slay her ; yet her pride shall die ! '
Again that hiss : instant the golden crown
Fell from her head !   In anger round she glared :—
Once more that hiss long-drawn, and in her hand
The goblet, shivered, stood !   She cast it down ;
She cried ; ' Since first I sat, a queen new-crowned,
Never such ignominy, or spleen of scorn
Hath mocked my greatness ! '   Fiercely rushed the chiefs
Against the aggressor.   Through the high-roofed woods
They saw him distant like a falling star
Kindling the air with speed.   Ere long, close by
He stood with sling high holden.   At its sound
Ever some great one died !

　　　　　　　　　The morrow morn
Cuchullain reached a lawn : tall autumn grass
Whitened within it ; but the Beech trees round
Were russet brown, the thorn-brakes berry-flushed :
Passing, he raised his spear, and launched it forth
Earthward : there stood it buried in the soil
Halfway, and quivering.   Loud Cuchullain laughed,
And cried, ' It quivers like the tail of swine
Gladdened by acorn feast ! ' then drew he rein
And with one sword-stroke felled a youngling Birch
And bound it to that spear, and on its bark
Silvery and smooth, graved with his lance's point
In Ogham characters the words, ' Beware !

Unless thou know'st what hand this Ogham traced
Twine yonder berries mid thy young bride's locks,
But spare to tempt that hand ! ' An hour passed by
And Meave had reached the spot.   Chief following chief
Drew near in turn ; yet none could drag from earth
That spear deep-buried.   Fergus laughed ; ' Let be
Connacians !   Task is here for Uladh's hand ! '
Then, standing in his car, he clutched the spear
And tugged it thrice.   The third time 'neath his feet
Down crashed the strong-built chariot to the ground.
He laughed !   The queen in anger cried, 'March on !'
The host advanced, disordered.   Foremost drave
Orloff, Meave's son.   That morning he had wed
A maid, the loveliest in his mother's court,
And yearned to prove his valour in her eyes.
Sudden he came to where Cuchullain stood
Pasturing his steeds with grass and flower forth held
In wooing, dallying hand.   Cuchullain said
' The queen's son this !   I will not harm the youth,'
And waved him to depart.   That stripling turned
Yet, turning, hurled his javelin.   As it flew
The swift one caught it ; poised it ; hurled it home :
It pierced that youth from back to breast ; he fell
Dead on the chariot's floor.   The steeds rushed on
Wind-swift ; and   reached the   camp.   There   sat   the
   queen

Throned in her car, listening the host's applause :
In swoon she fell, and lay as lie the dead.

Next morn again the invaders marched, nor knew
What foe was he who, mocking, thinned their ranks,
Trampled their pride ; who, lacking spear and car,
Viewless by day, by night a fleeting fire,
Dragged down their mightiest, in the death cry shrill
Drowning the revel.   Fergus knew the man,
Fergus alone ; nor yet divulged his name,
Oft muttering, ' These be men who fight for Bulls—
I war to shake a Perjurer from his throne,
And count no brave man foe.'   Again at feast
Ailill made question of the Red Branch Knights :
Fergus replied ; ' Cuchullain is their best :
I taught him arms !   Hear of his Knighting Day !

  ' Northward of Eman lies a pleasaunce green :
The Arch-Druid, Cathbad, gazer on the stars,
While there the youths contended, beckoned one
And whispered, ' Happy shall that stripling prove
Knighted this day !   Glorious his life, though brief !'
That hour Cuchullain stood beyond the wall
South of the city, yet that whisper heard !
He heard, and cried ; ' Enough one day of life
If great my deeds, and helpful !'   Swift of foot
He sped to Conor.   ' I demand, great king,
Knighthood this day, and knighthood at thy hand.'
But Conor laughed ; ' Not fifteen years are thine !

Withhold thyself yet three.'   That self-same hour
Old Cathbad entered, and his Druid clan,
And spake ; 'King Conor ! by my bed last night
Great Macha stood, the worship of our race,
Our strength in realms unseen.   "Arise," she said ;
" To Conor speed : to him report my will :
That youth knighted this day is mine Elect !
I, Macha, send him forth ! "

       ' She spake and passed :
Trembled the place like cliffs o'er ocean caves :
Like thunder underground I heard her wheels
In echoes slowly dying.

      ' Fixed and firm
King Conor stood.   Sternly he made reply :
' Queen Macha had her day and ruled : far down
Doubtless this hour she rules, or rules aloft :
I rule in Eman and this Uladh realm :
I will not knight a stripling ! '   Prophet-like
Up-towered old Cathbad, and his clan black-stoled.
This way and that they rolled prophetic bolts
Three hours ; and brake with warnings from the stars
And mandates from the synod of the Gods,
The king's resolve.   At last he cried, ' So be it !
Since Gods, like men, grow witless, be it so !
The worse for Eman, and great Macha's land—
Stand forth, my sister's son ! '   He spake and bound
The Geisa, and the edicts, and the vows

Of that dread Red Branch Order on the boy,
And gave him sword and lance.

      'An eye star-keen
That boy upon them fixed, and, each on each,
Smote them.   They snapt in twain.   Laughing, he cried,
'Good art thou, Uncle mine ; but these are base :
I need a warrior's weapons !'   Conor signed ;
Then brought his knaves ten swords, and lances ten :
Cuchullain eyed them each and snapt them all,
The concourse marvelling.   'Varlets,' cried the king,
'Bring forth my arms of battle !'   These in turn
Cuchullain proved : they brake not.   Up they dragged
A battle-car.   Cuchullain leaped therein :
With feet far set he spurned its brazen floor
That roared and sank in fragments.   Chariots twelve
Successive thus he vanquished.   'Uncle mine,
Good art thou,' cried the youth ; 'but these are base !'
King Conor signed, 'My car of battle !'   Leagh
The charioteer forth brought it with the steeds :
Cuchullain proved that war-car and it stood.
Careless he spake : 'So, well !   The car will serve !
Abide ye my return.'

      'He shook the reins :
He called the horses by their names well-known :
He dashed through Eman's gateway as a storm :
Far off a darksome wood and darksome tower
Frowned over Mallok's wave : therein abode

Three bandit chieftains, foes to man : well pleased
Those bandits eyed the on-rushing car, and youth,
Exulting in their prey : arrived, with gibes
He summoned them to judgment : forth they thronged,
They and their clan : he slew them with his sling,
The three ; and severed with his sword their heads,
And fixed them on the chariot's front.   His mood
Changed into mirthful : fleeter than the wind
Six stags went by him, stateliest of the herd ;
Afoot he chased them, caught them, bound them fast
Behind the chariot rail.   Birds saw he next
White as a foam-wreath of their native sea,
Spotting the glebe new turned.   A net lay near :
He caged them ; next he tied them to his car
Wide-winged, and wailing loud.   To Eman's towers
Returned he then with laughter : at its gate
The king, the chiefs, grey Druids, maids red-cloaked,
Agape to see him—on his chariot's front
The grim heads of those bandits ; in its rear
Those stags wide-horned ; and, high o'erhead the birds ! '
       The laughter ceasing, spake King Conor's son ;
' Recount the wonder of those fairy steeds
That drag Cuchullain's war-car ! '   Fergus then,
Despite Queen Meave, who plaited still her robe
With angry hectic hand, the tale began.
       ' Cuchullain paced the herbage thin that clothes
Slieve Fuad's summit.   On that airy height

A wan lake glittered, whitening in the blast,
Pale plains around it.   From beneath that lake
Emerged a horse foam-white !   Cuchullain saw,
And straightway round that creature's neck high-held
Locked the lithe arms no struggles could unwind.
That courser baffled clothed his strength with speed :
From cliff to cliff he sped ; cleared at a bound
Inlet, and rocky rift ; nor stayed his course,
Men say, till he had circled Erin's Isle.
Panting then lay he, on his conqueror's knee
Resting his head ; thenceforth that conqueror's friend,
His 'Liath Macha.'   Gentle-souled is she
'Sangland,' the wild one's comrade.   As the night
Sank on those huge red-berried woods of Yew
Loch Darvra's girdle, from beneath the wave
She issued, darker still.   Softly she paced,
As though with woman's foot, the grassy marge
In violets diapered, and laid her head
Upon Cuchullain's shoulder.   In his wars
Emulous those mated marvels drag his car :
In peace he yokes them never.'
                              Fergus rose :
' Night wanes,' he said, 'and tasks await my hand :'
Passing the throne he whispered thus the queen,
'The Hound of Uladh is your visitant
Both day and night.'   The cheek of Meave grew pale.

FRAGMENT II.

THE DEEDS OF CUCHULLAIN.

ARGUMENT.

FERGUS is sent to Cuchullain with gifts, and requires him to forsake
King Conor. This he will not do, yet consents to forbear Meave's
host till she has reached the border of Uladh, the queen engaging
that the warfare shall then be restricted to a combat between himself and a single champion sent against him day by day. Each day
Meave's champion is slain. Cailitin, lord of the Magic Clan,
counsels Meave to send against Cuchullain his best-loved friend
Ferdia; yet she sends, instead, Lok Mac Favesh. When he too
falls, Cailitin and his twenty-seven sons, all magicians, fling themselves upon Cuchullain to slay him. Cuchullain slays them. The
Mor Reega, the War-Goddess of the Gael, prophesies to him that
there yet awaits him the greatest of his trials. After ninety days of
combat Cuchullain's father brings him tidings that all Uladh lies
bound under a spell of imbecility.

THUS ever day by day, and night by night,
Through strength of him that mid the royal host
Passed, and re-passed like thought, the bravest fell ;
For ne'er against the inglorious or the small
That warrior raised his hand. Then Ailill spake ;
' Let Fergus seek that champion in the woods,
Gift-laden, and withdraw him from his king : '

But Fergus answered ; 'Sue and be refused !
That great one loves his country.   Heard ye never
How when King Conor's sin, that forfeit pledge
Plighted with Usnach's sons, had left the Accursed
Crownless, and Eman's bulwarks in the dust,
Her elders on Cuchullain worked, what time
He came my work of vengeance to complete ?
They said, " Cuchullain loves his land o'er all !
The man besides, though terrible to foes,
Is tender to the weak.   Through Eman's streets
Send ye proclaim, ' Will any holy Maid
To save the city take her station sole
On yonder bridge, at parting of the ways,
That city's Emblem-Victim, robed in black
Down from her girdle to the naked feet ;
Above that girdle this alone—the chains
Of Eman's gate, circling that virgin throat
And down at each side streaming?   It may be
That dread one will relent, pitying in her
Great Uladh's self despoiled of robe and crown,
Her raiment bonds and shame.'   Of Eman's maids
But one, the best and purest gave consent :
Alone she stood at parting of the ways :
While near and nearer yet that war-car drew
Wide-eyed she stood, death-pale : it stopp'd : she spake ;
  Eman, thy Mother, stands a widow now :

And many a famished babe that wrought no ill
Lies mid her ruins wailing." To the left
The warrior turned his steeds. The land was saved.'
    Then spake the kings confederate ; ' Hard albeit
That task, to draw Cuchullain from his charge,
Seek him, and proffer terms ! ' Fergus next morn
Made way through those sea-skirting woods, and cried
Three times, 'Setanta ; ' and Cuchullain heard
And knew that voice, and, beaming, issued forth,
And clasped his ancient master round the neck,
And led him to his sylvan cell. Therein
Long time they held discourse of ancient days
Heaven-fair through mist of years. The youthful host
Set forth their rural feast, whate'er the woods
And they that in them dwelt, swine-herds, and hinds,
Yielded, their best : nor lacked it minstrel strain,
Bird-song by autumn chilled, that brake through bou
Lit by unwarming sunshine. Banquet o'er,
Fergus his errand shewed, and named the gifts
By Ailill sent, and Meave. Cuchullain rose
And curtly answered ; ' Never will I break
My vow ; nor wrong the land ; nor sell my king :'
Fergus too royal was to hear surprised,
Or grieved, his friend's resolve, nor touched again
Upon that pact unworthy. Happier themes
Succeeded, mirthful some. Of these the last

L

Made sport of Ailill.   Fergus spake ; ' One night
To Meave's pavilion swift of foot I sped ;
War-tidings wait not.   Ailill from afar
Furtively followed, stung by jealous spleen.
The queen had passed into the inner tent ;
I sought her there.   In the outer Ailill marked
My sword, that morning thither sent, a loan,
For Meave had vowed with braided gems, her boast,
To out-brave its hilt.   His wrath was changed to joy !
He snatched it up ; he cried ; " Hail, forfeit mine !
Hail Eric just ! " and laughed his childish laugh.
Since then he neither frowns on me nor smiles :
He will not let me rule his foolish kings ;
Yet, deeming still my sword a charm 'gainst fate
Wears it.   An apter one for him I keep :
One day 'twill raise a laugh ! ' In graver mood
At parting Fergus spake ; ' For thee unmeet
That pact of Meave, though not for her : but thou
Conceal not, know'st thou meeter terms, and fit ? '
To whom Cuchullain ; ' Fergus, terms there be,
Other, and fitter.   I divulge them not :
Divine them he that seeks them ! ' On the morn
Fergus these things narrated to the chiefs
In synod met.   Then rose a recreant churl,
And thus gave counsel ; ' Lure Cuchullain here
On pretext fair ; and slay him at the feast ! '

Against that recreant Fergus hurled his spear,
And slew him, and continued, ' Hundreds six,
Our best, have perished, and our march is slow :
Now, warriors, hear my counsel, and my terms.
Cuchullain scorns your gifts—of such no more !
'Twixt southern Erin and my Uladh's realm,
Runs Neeth : across that river lies a ford ;
Speak to Cuchullain ; " By that ford stand thou,
Guarding thy land.   Against thee, day by day,
Be ours to send one champion—one alone :—
While lasts that strife forbear the host beside ! " '
    Then roared the kings a long and loud applause,
Since wise appeared that counsel : faith they pledged,
And sureties in the hearing of the Gods :
Likewise Cuchullain, when his friend returned,
Made answer ; ' Well you guessed ! a month or more
My strength will hold : meantime our Uladh arms.'
To seal that pact he sought the hostile camp,
And shared the banquet.   Wondering, all men gazed,
And maidens, lifted on the warriors' shields,
Gladdened, so bright that youthful face.   At morn
Meave, when the chief departed, kissed his cheek :
' Pity,' she said, ' that such a one should die ! '
The one sole time that Meave compassion felt.
    That eve Cuchullain drank the wave of Neeth,
And wading reached Murthemné's soil, his charge

And knelt, and kissed it.   As the sun declined
He clomb a rocky height, and northward gazed,
And cried ; ' Ye Red Branch warriors, haste !   I keep
The ford ; but who shall guard it when I die ? '
    Next morning by that stream the fight began,
Two champions face to face : and, every morn,
Rang out, renewed, that combat ; every eve
Again went up from that confederate host
The shout of rage.   Daily their bravest died ,
Thirty in thirty days.   Feerbraoth fell ;
And Natherandal, though the Druid horde
Above his javelins, carved at set of moon
From the ever-sacred holly stem, had breathed
Vain consecration, and with futile salve
Anointed them : confuted soon they sailed
In ignominy adown that seaward tide
With him that hurled them.   Eterconnel next,
Dalot, and Cuir.   Yet he who laid them low
Was beardless at the lip :—While thus they strove
A second month went by.
                    Such things beholding
The queen was moved ; and in her grew one day
Craving for Cruachan.   But on her ear
Rolled forth that hour the lowings of that Bull
Cuailgné's Donn : for he from Daré's house
Had heard, though far, the clamours of the host,

And answered rage with rage.   Then Meave resolved,
Though all my host should perish to a man
This foot shall tread no more my native plains
Save with that Bull in charge !
                              To her by night
Came Cailitin, who ever walked by night
Shunning mankind, and Fergus most of all,
Cailitin, father of the Magic Clan,
And thus addressed her ; ' Place in me thy trust !
I hate Cuchullain, for he hates my spells
Resting his hope on virtue.   In thy camp
Ferdia bides, a Firbolg feared of all.
Win him to meet Cuchullain.   They in youth
Were friends : to slay that friend will lay a hand
Icy as death upon Cuchullain's heart.
Ferdia dies—thus much mine art foreshews—
Then I, since magic spells have puissance most
Upon a soul depressed and body sick,
Fall on him with my seven and twenty sons,
Magicians all.   One are we : thence with one
May fight, thy pledge unflawed.   A drop of blood
Shed by our swords, though small as beetle's eye,
Costs him his life.'   Fiercely the queen replied,
' A Firbolg !   Never ! '   Cailitin resumed,
' Then send for Lok Mac Favesh ! '
                              With the morn

Mac Favesh sought her tent.   Direful his mien ;
Massive his stride ; his body brawny and huge ;
For, though of Gaelic race, the stock of Ir,
With him was mingled giant blood of old,
Wild blood of Nemedh's brood that hurled sea rocks
'Gainst the Fomorian.   Oft the advancing tide
Drowned both, in battle knit.   Before the queen
Boastful the sea-king laid his club, and spake :
' Queen, though to combat with a beardless boy
Affronts my name, my lineage, and my strength,
His petulance shall vex thine eye no more !
Uladh is thine to-morrow ! '   At the dawn
By hundreds girt, the great ones of his clan,
Down drave he to the ford, and onward strode
Trampling the last year's branches strewn hard by
That snapp'd beneath him.   Hides of oxen seven
Sustained the brazen bosses of his shield ;
And forth he stretched a hand that might have grasped
A tiger's throat and choked him.   O'er his helm
Hovered an imaged demon raven-black.
Cuchullain met him ; hours endured the strife,
That mountained strength triumphant now, anon
Cuchullain's might divine.   Then first that might
Was fully tasked.   Upon the bank that day
Stood up a Portent seen by none save him,
A Shape not human.   Terribly it fixed

On him alone its never-wandering eye ;
The dread Mor Reega, she that from the skies
O'er-rules the battle-fields, and sways at will
This way or that the sable tides of death.
He gazed ; and, though incapable of fear,
Awe, such as heroes feel, possessed his heart :
Its beatings shook his brain : his corporal mould
Throbbed as a branch against some river swift ;
And backward turned his hair like berried trails
Of thorn athwart the hedge.   Three several times
He saw her, yet fought on.   With beckoning hand
At last that Portent summoned from the main
A huge sea-snake : round him it twined its knots :
Then on Cuchullain fell the rage from heaven :
A sword-blow, and that vast sea-worm lay dead !
A sword uplifted, and Mac Favesh fell
Prone on the shuddering flood.   In death he cried,
' Lay me with forehead turned to Uladh's realm ;—
They shall not say that fugitive I died.'
Cuchullain wrought his will : then, bleeding fast,
Stood upright, leaning on his spear aslant ;
A warrior battle-wearied.

                      From the bank
Meantime, the dark magician, Cailitin,
He and his sons, with wide and greedy eyes,
That still, like one man's eyes, together moved,

Had watched that fight, counting each drop that fell
Down from Cuchullain's wounds. When faint he stood
At once their cry rang out like one man's cry ;
Like one their seven and twenty javelins flew :
As swift, Cuchullain caught them on his shield :
An instant more, and all that horde accursed
Was dealing with him. From the trampled ford
Went up a mist of spray that veiled that strife,
Though pierced by demon cries, and flash beside
Of demon swords. O'er it at last up-towered
On-borne, such power to blend have Spirits impure,
A single Form—as when o'er seas storm-laid
The watery column reels, and draws from heaven
The cloud, and drowns the ship—a single Form,
And Head, and Hand, clutching Cuchullain's crest :
Not wholly sank he. O'er that mist of spray
Glittered his sword. There fell a silence strange :
Slowly that mist dispersed ; and on the sands
That false Enchanter lay with all his sons
Black, bleeding bulks of death.

                          Amid them stood
Cuchullain ; near him, seen by him alone,
That dread Mor Reega, now benign. She spake :
' I hated thee, since less in me thy trust
Than in great Virtue's aid. I hate no more.

Be strong ! a trial waits thee heavier yet—
No man is friend of mine till trial-proved.'
   Yet sad at heart that eve Cuchullain clomb
His wonted rock, and faint with loss of blood,
And mused ; ' My strength must lessen day by day ;
And northward gazed, thus murmuring ; ' All too late
To save the land those Red Branch Knights will come
When I am dead—
My war-car, and my war-steeds are far off
And I am here alone.'   Through grief that night
He slept not ; for the Magic Clan had power,
Though dead, to lean above him as a cloud
Darkening his spirit.   Happy days gone by
They changed to grief and shame.

                   While thus he sat
He saw, not distant, on the forest floor,
In moonbeams clad, though moon was near him none,
A pure and princely presence.   Lithe his form
In youthful prime : chain armour round him clung
Bright as if woven of diamonds.   Glad his eye ;
Dulcet his voice as strain from Elfin glen
Far heard o'er waters.   Thus that warrior spake :
' My child, an ancestor of thine I come,
Great Ethland's son, in virtuous battle slain.
Among the Sidils now, and fairy haunts

Moon-lit, and under depths of lucent lakes,
Gladness I have who in my day had woe,
And youth perpetual though I died in age.
Repose thou need'st : for sixty days thine eyes
Have closed reluctant.   Sleep a three days' sleep
Whilst I thy semblance bearing meet thy foes.'
Thus spake the youth, then sang Lethean song,
And, straight, Cuchullain slept.   Three days gone by,
Again that vision came.   ' Arise,' he said :
The warrior rose ; and lo ! his wounds were healed :
Down to the river sped he.

              Waiting there
Stood up Iarion, champion of the queen,
There stood, nor thence returned.   Eochar next
Perished, then Tubar, Chylair, Alp, and Ord,
In all full ninety warriors.   Ninety days
Had fled successive since that strife began,
When, on the evening of the ninetieth day,
His strength entire, and victory eagle-winged
Fanning his ardent cheek, Cuchullain scaled
Once more that specular rock.   Within his heart
Spirit illusive that, with purpose veiled,
Oft tries the loftiest most, this presage sang
' Southward, not distant, thou shalt see them march
At last, that Red Branch Order, in their van
Thy Conal Carnach ! '   Other spectacle

Met him, a chariot small with horses small,
And, o er the axle bent, a small old man
Urging them feebly on.   It was his sire !
T'wards him Cuchullain rushed : the old man wept,
For gladness wept, and afterwards for woe,
Kissing the wounds unnumbered of his son :
Reverent, Cuchullain led him to his cell ;
Reverent, he placed before him wine and meat ;
Nor questioned yet.   The old man satisfied,
Garrulity returned, though less than once,
Now quelled by patriot passion.   Thus he spake :—
'Setanta ! son of mine ! I bring ill news :
Uladh is mad ; the Red Branch House is mad :
We two are mad ; and all the world are mad,
Mad as thy mother !   Through the realm I sped :
A mist hung o'er it heavy, and on her sons
Imbecile spirit, and a heartless mind,
And base soul-sickness.   Evermore I cried,
" Arise ! the stranger's foot is on your soil :
They come to stall their horses in your halls ;
To slay your sons ; enslave your spotless maids ;
Alone my son withstands them ! "   Shrewd of eye
Men answered ; " Merchant ; see thy wares be sound !
No lack-wits we ! "   Old seers I saw that decked
Time-honoured foreheads with a jester's crown :
I saw an ollamb trample under foot

His sacred Oghams : next I saw him grave
His own blear image on the tide-washed sands,
Boasting, "The unnumbered ages here shall stoop
Honouring true Wisdom's image."   Shepherds set
The wolf to guard their fold.   The wittol bade
The losel lead his wife to feast and dance :
Young warriors looked on maids with woman's eyes.
I drave to Daré's Dûn : his loud-voiced sons
Adored the Donn Cuailgné as their sire,
And called their sire a calf.   To Iliach's tower
I sped : he answered ; "What ! the foe ! they come !
Climb we yon apple trees, and garner store !
Wayfarers need much victual !"   Onward next
To Sencha's castle :—On the roof he knelt,
Self-styled the kingdom's chief astrologer,
Waiting the unrisen stars.   To Olchar's Dûn
I journeyed : wrapp'd in rags the strong man lay,
Thin from long fast ; with eyelids well nigh closed :
Not less beneath them lay a gleaming streak :
"Awake me not," he said : "a dormouse I !
Till peace returns I simulate to sleep."
I sought the brothers Nemeth : one his eyes
Bent on the smoke-wreath from his chimney's top,
One on the foam-streak wavering down the stream ;
While each a finger raised, and said "Tread light !
Our earth is grass o'er glass !"   I sought the mart :

Men babbled ; "Bid the Druids find the king !"
I sought the Druids' College : in a hall
Reed-strewn to smother sound they held debate
On Firbolg and Dedannan contracts pledged
Ere landed first the Gael.   The Red Branch House
Was changed to hospital ; and knights full-armed
Nodded o'er lepers' beds.   I sought the king :
From hall deserted on to hall I roamed :
I found him in his armoury walled around
With mail of warriors dead.   There stood, or lay,
The chiefs by Uladh worshipp'd.   Nearest, crouched
Great Conal Carnach patting of his sword
Like nurse that lulls an infant.   On his throne
Sat Conchobar in miniver and gold :
His eyes were on his grandsire's shield that breathed
At times a sigh athwart the steel-lit gloom :
Around his lips an idiot's smile was curled :
" What will be will be," spake the king at last :
" All things go well." '
     Thus Saltain told his tale :
One thing he told not—how, a moment's space,
The passion of an old man's scorn had wrought
Deliverance strange for that astonished throng,
High miracle of nature.   He, the man
Despised since youth, the laughter of the crowd,
Himself restored to youth by change like death,

Had rolled his voice abroad, a mighty voice ;
They heard it : from their trance they burst : they stood
Radiant once more with mind !   They stood till died
The noble anger's latest echo.   Then
That mist storm-riven put forth once more its hand,
And downward dragged its prey.

                           Upon his feet
Cuchullain sprang, his father's tale complete :
That rage divine which gave him strength divine
Had fallen on him from heaven.   He raised his hands,
And roared against the synod of the Gods
That suffer shames below.   Beyond the stream
That host confederate heard and armed in haste,
And slept that night in armour.   Far away
Compassion touched the strong hearts of the Gods,
The strongest most—Mor Reega's.   Ere that cry
Had left its last vibration on the air
High up the Battle-Goddess, adamant-mailed,
Was drifting over Uladh.   Eman's towers
Flashed back her helmet's beam.   With lifted spear
She smote the brazen centre of her shield
Three times ; and thunder, triple-bolted, rolled
Three times from sea to sea.   The spell was snapp'd :
Humanity returned to man !   The first
Who woke was Leagh, Cuchullain's charioteer :
Forth from the opprobrious mist he passed like ship

That cleaves the limit of some low marsh-fog
And sweeps into main ocean.   Forth he rushed —
Forth to Cuchullain's chariot-house, and dragged
Abroad that war-car feared of man and yoked
White Liath Macha, and his comrade black,
And dashed adown the vacant, echoing streets,
And passed the gateway towers : the warders slept :
Beyond them, propp'd against the city wall,
A cripple crunched his mouldering crust.   Still on
He rushed, the reins forth shaking and the scourge,
Clamouring and crying ; ' Haste, Cuchullain's steeds !
On Liath Macha !   Sable Sangland on !
Your master needs you !   Aye ! ye know it now !
The blood-red nostril smells the fight far off !
On to Murthemné, and Cuailgné's hills,
And Neeth's remembered ford ! '   Unseen he drave ;
So slowly, clinging still to brake and rock,
And oft re-settling, vanished from the land
The insane mist.   That hurricane of wheels
Not less was heard by men who nothing saw :
On stony plain, in hamlet, and in vale :—
They muttered as in sleep ; ' Deliverance comes.'

FRAGMENT III.

THE COMBAT AT THE FORD.

ARGUMENT.

QUEEN MEAVE sends her herald to Ferdïa the Firbolg, requiring him to engage with Cuchullain in single combat. Ferdïa refuses to fight against his ancient friend ; yet, later he attends a royal banquet given in his honour ; and there, being drawn aside through the witcheries of the Princess Finobar, he consents to the fight. The charioteer of Ferdïa sees Cuchullain advancing in his war-car to the Ford, and, rapt by a prophetic spirit, sings his triumph. For two days the ancient friends contend against each other with reluctance and remorse : but on the third day the battle-rage bursts fully forth : and on the fourth, Cuchullain, himself pierced through with wounds innumerable, slays Ferdïa by the Gae-Bulg. He lays his friend upon the bank, at its northern side, and, standing beside him, sings his dirge.

MEANTIME the queen, ere dawned that ninetieth morn,
Mused, ill at ease ; ' Daily my people die,
And many a stormy brow on me is bent :—
What if they turn on me like starving hounds
That rend their huntsman ?' In her ear once more
Sounded the word of Cailitin ; ' The man
To fight Cuchullain is the man he loves :

His death were death to both.'   Then came the kings
Confederate, saying ; 'Send Ferdia forth !
Ferdia is the mightiest of our host :
Ferdia is Cuchullain's chief of friends :
Westward of Alba in the Isle of Skye
Scatha, that rock-browed northern warrioress,
In amplest lore of battles trained them both :
Except the Gae-Bulg, every feat of arms
Is known to each alike.'

                The queen gave way :
She sent her herald to the man she scorned
With offers huge, tract vaster than his own
Not barren like his mountains billow-beat,
But laughing in the lap of Ai's plains ;
A war-car deftly carved and ribbed with brass ;
And, for his clansmen, raiment of all dyes,
Twelve suits.   A stalwart man, yet fair as strong
The Firbolg towered, dark-eyed, dark-haired, pale-faced,
Unlike the Gael.   Melodious was his voice
But deeper than a lion's.   Ceaseless thought
On immemorial wrongs—he brooded still
O'er glories of Moytura, and Tailltenn,
Their great assemblies, and their solemn games,
And kingly graves—had cast upon his brow
Perpetual shade ; and ever, on the march,
If high on crags there stood some Gaelic tomb

Wind-worn a thousand years, he passed it by
With face averse, muttering, 'New men !   New men !
We note not such !'   The herald's task discharged,
He answered thus, not turning ; 'Tell your queen
That I, a Firbolg, serve, but not for hire,
A cause not mine.   Cuchullain is my friend :
Better I died than he !'

       O'er-awed though wroth
The queen despatched in statelier embassage
Three warriors, and three ollambs, and three bards :
With reverence they addressed him.   'Chief and Prince !
True prince, though scion of a house deject,
The queen, who judges all men by their deeds,
This day hath in thine honour made a feast
And sues to it thy presence.   Kings alone
Partake that banquet ; Ailill first, and she
Of princesses the fairest, Finobar !'
Scornful the Firbolg answered ; 'Finobar !
She whose bright face hath frosted with death's white
Full four score faces of war-breathing men
Sent to that Ford successive !   Let it be !
Tell them I join their feast : tell them beside
Their bribe shall prove base gold !'

        In mantle blue
Clasped by a silver torque, and silver belt
Enringed with silver rings innumerable

That evening from his tent Ferdia strode
With large attendance. Ailill and the queen
Received him on their threshold. At the board
Princes alone had place. High up, o'er each
Glittered upon the wall his blazoned shield.
King Ailill placed Ferdia on his right ;
Beyond him sat the Princess. In her ear
Her mother whispered as she neared that seat :
She answered with her eyes.
                                        Well stricken harp
Gladdened that festive throng ; and many a tale,
The rage of hunger lessening by degrees,
Ailill recounted of the heroic past,
When, youthful yet, he ranged 'mid friends and foes
Such men as breathed no longer. Servitors
Brimmed oft the goblets ; and Ferdia's brow,
As song to song succeeded, tale to tale,
Remitted its first sternness. Finobar
Unconsciously had dropp'd her jewell'd hand
Not far from his : her large and dusky eyes,
Shyly at first from his withdrawn, at last
Full frankly met them : on her lips the smile
Increased, though waveringly, then waned, not died,˙
And in it sadness mingled as she spake :
' But late yon harper told us of a dream—
My earliest of remembered dreams was sad ;

M 2

I saw some princess of your earlier stock
Whose lover late had perished, slain in fight
By ours, methought them recent.   At her feet—
Why there I scarcely know—I made lament :
" All thou hast lost for thy sake I renounce :
For me, like thee, no bridal rites forever !
Dead on thy marriage garland lies mine own ;
For lo ! the stain accursed is on our sword :
Thy race came first : this Island should be theirs ! "
Ferdia listened ; and the icy pride
Thawed in his bosom.   With a sudden change
The jubilant music into martial soared,
Wild battle-chaunt.   Upon the warrior's hand
Still nigh to hers, there lay a scar.   With eye
Reverently dewed the princess gazed thereon :
' Aye, of your war-deeds I have heard so long,
It seems as though since childhood—Whence that wound?
What battle left it there ?   What sister bound it ?
I would that sister were my sister too,
Partaker of my heart, my hope, my life : ·
I have no youthful friend ! '   She paused :—again
But now with paler cheek, and hurried, spake :
' Beware my mother !   She would send you forth
Her knight to meet Cuchullain !   Shun that man !
Cuchullain spares not : four score warriors dead
Avouch it.   Chief of Gaels is he !   Ah me !

The last great battle 'twixt the old race and new
Would find the same sad ending as the first.'
The Firbolg frowned : she faltered, 'Am I false,
False to my race '—and tears were in her voice—
' False to my race, who cannot wish such ending ? '
She paused ; again she questioned of his wars :
He told her of his sire's.   Like one who thinks
Not speaks, she murmured low ; ' A soothsayer
Thus warned my mother—I was then a child—
" Bring not that maid to war-fields !   She shall die
Grieving for some dead warrior." '

                              Changed once more
The martial songs to amorous and of mirth,
And once again the torches' golden flame
Laughed on the cup new-brimmed.   Again she spake,
That lovesome one, ' I love not songs of love !
Better the war-song !   Best, methinks, of all
That lullaby half war and sorrow half
Breathed by some bride while o'er her wounded lord
Softly descends the sleep :—so softly sank
Cold dews of evening on this flower still wet.'
She took it from her breast, and held it near :
He smelt it ; kissed it ; kept it.   With a smile
She added ; ' For your sister ?   Have you one ?
If so, 'tis likely she resembles me :
They chide me oft ; " No Gaelic face is thine,

Dark-eyed, dark-browed, a rebel since its birth ! " '
She ceased ; again she spake : ' Even now, methinks,
That lullaby I spake of I can hear !
Is it for thee, my friend, or Cuchullain ? '
That hand, of flower amerced, drew nearer yet
To his.   That smile had passed.   Tearful she turned
On him those luminaries of love and death,
Her eyes, like stars in midnight waters glassed ;
Turned them, but spake no longer.   Through his brain
Shivered their shrouded lustre ; through his blood :
The sanguine currents from the warrior's heart
Long sad, to female sympathies unused,
Drank up at once that splendour, and the tears
That splendour's strange eclipse.

                                    And yet, that hour,
Seen in some lonelier region of his soul
Another presence, O how different, stood !
Again, that hour, he saw those guileless eyes,
Blue as the seas they gazed on ; saw once more
That hair like winter sunshine, brow snow-white,
That unvoluptuous form and virginal,
That love-unwakened breast with love for all,
Those hands that knew not what their touch conferred,
Those blithesome, wave-washed, scarce divided feet :—
The huge cliff smiled upon her ; seemed to say,
' Ah little nursling mine !   Ah tender child

Of winds and rocks untender ! '

                      Had he loved ?
Sadness is celibate and eremite :
His converse long had been with injuries past,
In Scatha's isle with frowning crags and clouds—
Aye, but with one beside, a friend, his nearest,
Who loved that maid, and sued her grace. Ferdia
Had never spoken love ; nor thought, ' I love : '
And yet, that hour, was false.

                      A hundred harps
Rang out together, and the feast was o'er :
Murmured the rose-red lips ; but what they said
He heard not. Mournfully at last withdrew
Those eyes, like eyes fated thenceforth to bear
One image on till death. She joined her mother.
The queen, as he departed, took his hand :
Alone they stood : she spake : ' That noble scorn
Which spurned a bribe, approves a Firbolg's worth :
'Twas Ailill sent that herald. 'Twas not I.
I know you now, and proffer royal terms
Confirmed by guarantee of all our kings :
Accept this combat ; and the princess wed !
Ferdia ! I have made that offer thrice
To three dead warriors with the king's consent,
Never till now with hers ! '

                      He pledged his word :

The battle day was fixed ; the morrow morn :
She took that glittering torque whose splendours clasped
Her mantle red ; with it his mantle bound :
Then with attendance to his tent he passed.

    Meantime, that night within his forest lair
In dreams Cuchullain lay, and saw in dreams,
Not recent fights, but ocean and that isle
Where with Ferdia he had dwelt in youth,
With Scatha—and another.   And in dream
He mused ; 'The dearest of my friends survives :
These wars will pass ; Ferdia then and I
Thenceforth are one for aye !'   That self-same hour
Sadly from troubled sleep the Firbolg woke,
Murmuring, as one in trance, 'Against my friend !
Against my only friend !'   With gloomy brows
His clansmen watched him arming.   One sole man
They feared ; that man Cuchullain.   Morn the while
Was dawning, though nor glowing cheek she raised
Nor ardent eyes, with silver wand not gold
Striking the unkindling portals of the East ;
And, ere the sun had risen, Ferdia bathed
Three times his forehead in the frosty stream ;
And bade attend his charioteer ; and drave
Begirt by stateliest equipage of war
Down to the river's brim.   In regal pomp
The host confederate followed, keen to watch

With Meave, and Ailill, and with Finobar,
All passions of a fight unmatched till then ;
While clustered here and there, on rock or mound,
Minstrel and food-purveyor groom and leech
With healing herbs, and charms.
                              The sun arose
And smote the forest roof dew-saturate
As onward dashed through woodlands to the Ford
Cuchullain's war-car.   Nearer soon it rolled
Crushing the rocks.   Above those wondrous steeds
That Great One glittered through the mist of morn,
Splendour gloom-veiled.   Ferdia's charioteer
Half heard, half saw him.   Spirit-rapt, yet awed,
Perforce thus sang he standing near the marge.
  ' I hear the on-rushing of the car !   I see
There throned that warrior not of mortal mould
Swathed in the morning.   Dreadful are his wheels ;
Dreadful as breaker arched, when on its crest
Stands Fear, and Fate upon the rock-strewn shore :
But not sea-rocks they crush, those brazen wheels,
But realms, and peoples, and the necks of men.
  ' I see the war-car !   Terrible it comes,
Four-peaked ; and o'er those peaks a shadowy pall
Pavilioning dim crypt and caves of death :
I see it by the gleam of spears high held,
The glare of circling Spirits.   Lo ! the same

I saw far northward drifting, months gone by,
Ere yet that madness quelled the northern land.'
　　　Then cried Ferdia, stationed where huge trees
Shut out unwelcome vision : ' For a bribe
Thou seest these portents, singing of my death ! '
　　　Once more, in agony prophetic, he—
' The man within that car is Uladh's Hound !
What hound?　No stag-hound of the storm-swept hills :
No watch-hound watching by a merchant's store :
The hound he is that tracks the steps of doom ;
The hound of realms o'er-run, and hosts that fly ;
The hound that laps the blood ! '
　　　　　　　　　　　　　　Again he sang ;
' The Hound of Uladh is a hound with wings ;
A hound man-headed !　Yea, and o'er that head
Victory and empire, like two eagles paired
Sail onward, tempest-pinioned.　Endless morn
Before him fleeting over seas and lands,
With shaft retorted lights his chariot-beam.
That chariot stays not, turns not : on it comes,
Like torrent shooting from a tall cliff's brow,
Level long time ; then downward borne ! '
　　　　　　　　　　　　　　　　' A bribe ! '
Once more Ferdia cried ; ' A bribe ! a lie !
Traitor ! for Ailill's gold and gold of Meave,
Thou sing'st thy master's death-song ! '

By the stream
Cuchullain stood : not yet he knew his foe ;
That foe who slowly to the Ford advanced
Full panoplied, and in his hand a spear.
Long gazed they each on each. Cuchullain spake :
'Welcome howe'er thou com'st, Ferdia ! Once
In Scatha's isle far otherwise thou camest
Morn after morn with tidings fresh of war
Plaything and pastime of our brother swords.
This day thou com'st invader of my land
Murthemné, bulwark broad of Uladh's realm ;
Thou com'st to burn my cities, spoil my flocks—
A change there is, Ferdia !' Stern of brow
The Firbolg answered ; 'Friends we were ; not peers :
The younger thou. 'Twas thine to yoke my steeds ;
Arm me for fight. A stripling hopes this day
With brandished spear to make a mountain flee !
Son of the Gael ! long centuries since, thy race
Trampled my race :—their vengeance hour is near ;
I bid thee to depart !' To him his friend ;
'Ferdia, in the old days on Scatha's Isle
Thou wert my tribe, my household-stock, my race !
Questioned I then on battle-plain, or when
On frosty nights we couched beneath one rug,
Ancestral claims, traditions of the clan ?
A change there is, Ferdia !'

Thus with words
Or mild, or stern in hope to save not slay,
Those friends contended.   Sternest was the man
Whose conscience most aggrieved him.

'' To this Ford
Thou cam'st the first, old comrade ! choice of arms
Is therefore thine by right.'   Cuchullain spake :
Ferdia chose the javelin.   Arrow-swift,
While still the charioteers brought back the shaft,
The missiles flew.   Keen-eyed as ocean bird
That, high in sunshine poised, glimpses his prey
Beneath the wave, and downward swooping slays him,
Each watched the other's movements, if an arm
Lifted too high, or buckler dropp'd too low
Left bare a rivet.   Long that fight endured :
Three times exhausted sank their hands : three times
They sat on rocks for respite, each the other
Eyeing askance, not silent ; ' Lo the man
Who shields an ox-like or a swine-like race
That strikes no blow itself !' or thus ; 'Ah pledge
Of amity eterne in old time sworn !
Ferdia, vow thy vow henceforth to maids !
The man-race nothing heeds thee !'

Evening fell
And stayed perforce that combat.   Slowly drew
The warriors near ; and as they noted, each,

The other bleeding, in its strength returned
The friendship unextinct : round either's neck
That other wound his arms and kissed him thrice :
That night their coursers in the self-same field
Grazed, side by side : that night their charioteers
With rushes gathered from the self-same stream
Made smooth their masters' beds, then sat themselves
By the same fire.   Of every healing herb
That lulled his wounds Cuchullain sent the half
To staunch Ferdia's ; while to him in turn
Ferdia sent whate'er of meats or drinks
Held strengthening power or cordial, to allay
Distempered nerve or nimble spirit infuse,
In equal portions shared.

                  The second morn
They met at sunrise :—' Thine the choice of arms ;'
The Firbolg spake ; the Gael made answer ; 'Spears !'
Then leaped the champions on their battle-cars
And launched them into battle.   Dire their shock
In fiery orbits wheeling now ; anon
Wheel locked in wheel.   Profounder wounds by far
That day than on the first the warriors gored,
Since closer was the fight.   With laughing lip
Not less that eve Cuchullain sang the stave
That chides in war ' Fomorian obstinacy :'
Again at eve drew near they, slower now

For pain, and interwove fraternal arms :
Again their coursers in the self-same field
Grazed side by side, and from the self-same stream
Again their charioteers the rushes culled :
Again they shared alike both meats and drinks,
Again those herbs allaying, o'er their wounds
With incantations laid.

              Forlorn and sad
Peered the third morning o'er the vaporous woods,
The wan grey river with its floating weed,
And bubble unillumined.   From the marge
Cuchullain sadly marked the advancing foe :—
' Alas, my brother ! beamless is thine eye ;
The radiance lives no longer on thy hair ;
And slow thy step.'   The doomed one answered calm,
' Cuchullain, slow of foot, but strong of hand
Fate drags his victim to the spot decreed :
The choice to-day is mine : I choose the sword.'
    So spake the Firbolg ; and they closed in fight :
And straightway from his heart to arm and hand
Rushed up the strength of all that buried race
By him so loved !   Once more it swelled his breast :
In majesty re-clothed each massive limb,
And flashed in darksome light of hair and eye
Resplendent as of old.   Surpassing deeds
They wrought, while circled meteor-like their swords,

Or fell like heaven's own bolt on shield or helm.
Long hours they strove till morning's purer gleams
Vanished in noon.   Sharper that day their speech ;
For, in the intenser present, years gone by
Hung but like pallid, thin, horizon clouds
O'er memory's loneliest limit.   Evening sank
Upon the dripping groves and shuddering flood
With rainy wailings.   Not as heretofore
Their parting.   Haughtily their mail they tossed
Each to his followers.   In the self-same field
That night their coursers grazed not ; neither sat
Their charioteers beside the self-same fire :
Nor sent they, each to other, healing herbs.

    Ere morn the Firbolg drank the strength of dreams
Picturing his race's wrong ; and trumpet blasts
Went o'er him blown from fields of ancient wars :
And thus he mused, half-wakened ; 'Not for Meave ;
Not for the popular suffrage ; not for her
That maid who fain had held me from the snare,
Fight I that fight whose end shall crown this day :
O race beloved, this day your vengeance dawns
Red in the East !   The mightiest of the Gaels
Goes down before me !   What if both should die ?
So best !   Thus too the Firbolg is avenged ! '
Thus mused he.   Stately from his couch he rose,
And armed himself, sedate.   Upon his breast

He laid, in iron sheathed, a huge, flat stone,
For thus he said, 'Though many a feat of arms
Is mine, from Scatha learned, or else self-taught,
The Gae-Bulg is Cuchullain's!' On his head
He fixed his helm, and on his arm his shield
Sable as night, with fifty bosses bound,
All brass ; the midmost like a noontide sun.

    Cuchullain eyed him as he neared the Ford,
And spake to Leagh ; 'This day, if slack of hand
Thou notest me, or wearied, hurl, as wont,
Sharp storm of arrowy railing from thy lips
That so the battle-anger from on high
May flame on me.' The choice of arms was his :
He chose 'the Ford-Feat.' On the Firbolg's brow
A shadow fell :—'All weapons there,' he mused,
'Have place alike : if on him falls the rage
He will not spare the Gae-Bulg!'

                Well they knew,
Both warriors, that the fortunes of that day
Must end the conflict ; that for one, or both,
The sun that hour ascending shone his last :
Therefore all strength of onset till that hour
By either loosed or hoarded, craft of fight
Reined in one moment but to spring the next
Forward in might more terrible, compared
With that last battle was a trivial thing ;

Whilst every weapon, javelin, spear, or sword,
Lawful alike that day, scattered abroad
Huge flakes of dinted mail ; from every wound
Bounded the life-blood of a heart athirst
For victory or for death.   The vernal day
Panted with summer ardours, while aloft
Noontide, a fire-tressed Fury, waved her torch,
Kindling the lit grove and its youngling green
From the azure-blazing zenith.   As the heat
So waxed the warriors' frenzy.   Hours went by :
That day they sought not rest on rock or mound ,
Held no discourse.   Slowly the sun declined ;
And as wayfarers oft when twilight falls
Advance with strength renewed, so they, refreshed,
Surpassed their deeds at morning.   With a bound
Cuchullain, from the bank high springing, lit
Full on the broad boss of Ferdia's shield,
His dagger-point down turned.   With spasm of arm
Instant the Firbolg from its sable rim
Cast him astonished.   Upward from the Ford
Again Cuchullain reached that shield : again
With spasm of knee Ferdia flung him far,
While Leagh in scorn reviled him : ' As the flood
Shoots on the tempest's blast its puny foam ;
The oak-tree casts its dead leaf on the wave ;
The mill-wheel showers its spray ; the shameless woman

N

Hurls on the mere that babe which was her shame,
So hurls he forth that fairy-child bewitched
Whom men misdeemed for warrior ! '

                   Then from heaven
Came down upon Cuchullain, like the night,
The madness-rage.   The Foes confronted met :
Shivered their spears from point to haft : their swords
Flashed lightnings round them. Fate-compelled, their feet
Drew near, then reached that stream which backward
    fled
Leaving its channel dry.   While raged that fight
Cuchullain's stature rose, huge bulk, immense,
Ascending still : as high Ferdīa towered
Like Fomor old, or Nemed from the sea,
Those shields, their covering late from foot to helm,
Shrinking, so seemed it, till above them beamed
Shoulders and heads.   So close that fight, their crests
That waved defiance, mingled in mid air ;
While all along the circles of their shields,
And all adown their swords, viewless for speed
Ran, mad with rage, the demons of dark moors
And war-sprites of the valleys, Bocanachs
And Banacahs, whose scream, so keen its edge,
Might shear the centuried forest as the scythe
Shears meadow grass.   To these in dread response
Thundered far off from sea-caves billow-beat

And halls rock-vaulted 'neath the eternal hills,
That race Tuatha, giant once, long since
To pigmy changed, that forge from molten ores
For aye their clanging weapons, shield or spear,
On stony anvils, waiting still their day
Of vengeance on the Gael.   That tumult scared
The horses of the host of Meave that brake
From war-car or the tethering rope, and spread
Ruin around.   Camp-followers first, then chiefs
Innumerable were dragged along, or lay
'Neath broken axle, dead.   The end was nigh :
Cuchullain's shield splintered upon his arm
Served him no more ; and through his fenceless side
Ferdia drave the sword.   Then first the Gael
Hurled forth this taunt ; 'The Firbolg, bribed by Meave,
Has sold his ancient friend !'   Ferdia spake,
'No Firbolg he, the man in Scatha's Isle,
That won a maid, then left her !'   Backward stepp'd
Cuchullain paces three : he reached the bank ;
He uttered low ; 'The Gae-Bulg !'   Instant, Leagh
Within his hand had lodged it.   Bending low,
Low as that stream, the war-game's crowning feat,
He launched it on Ferdia's breast.   The shield,
The iron plate beneath, the stone within it,
Like shallow ice-films 'neath a courser's hoof
Burst.   All was o'er.   To earth the warrior sank :

N 2

Dying, he spake : 'Not thine this deed, O friend—
'Twas Meave who winged that bolt into my heart !'
    Then ran Cuchullain to that great one dead,
And raised him in his arms, and laid him down
Beside the Ford, but on its northern bank,
Not in that realm by Ailill swayed and Meave :
Long time he looked the dead man in the face ;
Then by him fell in swoon.   'Cuchullain, rise !
The men of Erin be upon thee !   Rise !'
Thus Leagh.   He answered, waking ; 'Let them come !
To me what profit if I live or die ?
The man I loved is dead !'
                                But by the dead
Cuchullain stood ; and thus he made lament :
'Ferdia !   On their head the curse descend
Who sent thee to thy death !   We meet no more ;
Never while sun, and moon, and earth endure.
    'Ferdia !   Far away in Scatha's isle
A great troth bound us and a vow eterne
Never to raise war-weapons, each on each :—
'Twas Finobar that snared thee !   She shall die.
    'Ferdia ! dearer to my heart wert thou
Than all beside if all were joined in one :
Dear was thy clouded face, and darksome eye ;
Thy deep, sad voice ; thy words so wise and few ;
Dear was thy silence : dear thy slow, grave ways,
Not boastful like the Gael's.'

Silent he stood
While Leagh in reverence from the dead man's breast
Loosened his mail.   There shone the torque of Meave:
There where the queen had fixed it yet it lay.
Cuchullain clutched it.   'Ha! that torque I spurned!
Dark gem ill-lifted from the seas of Death!
Swart planet bickering from the heavens of Fate!
With what a baleful beam thou look'st on me!
'Twas thou, 'twas thou, not I, that slew'st this man '—
He dashed it on the rock, and with his heel
Smote it to fragments.

        Then, as one from trance
Waking, once more he spake : 'Oh me—oh me,
That I should see that face so great and pale!
To-day face-whitening death is on that face ;
And in my hand my sword :—'tis crimson yet.
That day when he and I triumphed in fight
By Formait's lake o'er Scatha's pirate foes
The woman fetched a beaker forth of wine,
And made us drink it both ; and made us vow
Friendship eterne.   O friend, my hand this day
Tendered a bloody beaker to thy lip.'

   Again he sang ; 'Queen Meave to Uladh's bound
Came down ; and dark the deed that grew thereof ;
Came down with all the hosting of her kings ;
And dark the deed that grew thereof.   We two
Abode with Scatha in her northern isle,

Her pupils twinned.   The sea-girt warrioress
That honoured few men honoured us alike :
We ate together of the self-same dish :
We couched together 'neath the self-same shield :
Now living man I stand, and he lies dead !'
   He raised again his head : once more he sang :
' Each battle was a game, a jest, a sport
Till came, fore-doomed, Ferdia to the Ford.
I loved the warrior though I pierced his heart.
Each battle was a game, a jest, a sport
Till stood, self-doomed, Ferdia by the Ford.
Huge lion of the forestry of war ;
Fair, central pillar of the House of Fame ;
But yesterday he towered above the world :
This day he lies along the earth, a shade.'

FRAGMENT IV

THE INVASION OF ULADH.

ARGUMENT.

CUCHULLAIN lies long in the forest nigh to death from his wounds, and yet more through grief for Ferdia. The queen crosses the Ford into Uladh, and captures the Donn Cuailgné. The confederate kings fall out among themselves; Meave summons a war council; whereupon there bursts forth a second contention between them and the Exile-Band. She makes the circuit of all Uladh; yet enacts nothing memorable. Lastly she marches against Eman, its metropolis, but slowly, being encumbered by her spoil. Uladh rouses itself daily out of its trance of imbecility. The death of Ketherne. Finobar is fain to draw Rochad to the cause of her mother, but fails. Her fate. The queen, falling into despondency, re-crosses the frontier.

SILENCE amid the wide, confederate camp :
No clang of sword or shield ; no warrior's tread
Striding to Meave with battle-gage down flung
For him who kept the Ford. But when six days
Were past, and none had seen that threatening helm,
There went abroad a rumour, 'he is dead :'
Then sped to her six champions claiming fight :
Whom from her presence spurning, Meave advanced

With all her host o'er Uladh's frontier line
By Daré's castle and the ill-omened gate
Whereon high-seated Daré's Fool had hurled
Against her scorn and gibe.   As Meave drew near
Forth rolled the bellowing of Cuailgné's Donn,
Cause of that war.   King Daré's sons had fled ;
But in the gate-way stood their old, grey sire,
Alone, and slew the first that entrance made :
The rest dashed in upon him, and he died.

　Six days, and in Cuchullain's cell no change—
The bud grew large ; the earlier violet died ;
He neither spake nor moved.   His wounds were deep :
Deeper his grief ; and stronger thence their power
Though dead, that c'an accursed of Cailitin,
With ghostly spells darkening the warrior's heart :
As lie the dead, he lay.

　　　　　　　　　One eve, what time
The setting sun levell'd through holly brakes
Unnumbered dagger-points of jewel'd light
And 'neath the oak-stem burned a golden spot,
Leagh, standing near his couch, reproached him thus ;
' In time of old the greatness of thy spirit
Had ever strength to salve thy corporal griefs :
But now through coward heart thou makest no fight,
Dying as old men die.'   Cuchullain heard ;
But answered nought.

　　　　　　　Next day, while near them buzzed
At noon the gilded insect swarm, he spake ;
' While lived Ferdia wounds to thee were jest ;
Thy grief it is that drags thee to the pit ;
Grief ; and for what ?　Of treasons worse is none
Than sorrow when thy country's foe is dead !
Not man is he, the man who dies of grief.'
He spake : Cuchullain fixed a vacant eye
On that sad, wrathful face.

　　　　　　　　　Then hastened Leagh
To where those giant coursers, side by side,
Stood tethered mid green grass and meadow-sweet
Within a lawn ; and led them to a stream,
And bade them drink ; and later led them home ;
And placed their corn before them, and they ate :
Next spake he ; ' Horses ye ; and yet ye know
To eat at need, while men self-sentenced starve ! '
Thus of that man whom most he loved on earth
He made complaint.　Liath, the lake's white son,
Tossed high his head in anger.　By his side
Sangland, his dusky comrade, sadly ate,
Moistening with tears her barley.

　　　　　　　　　　Late that eve
Cuchullain beckoned Leagh ; ' To Conor speed :
Speak thus ; " Put on thine arms and save thy land
Since now the Hound that kept thy gate is dead :—

Make no delay !"'   At midnight Leagh went forth
Though loth to leave his master to the care
Of cowherd rude, or swineherd.   Tenderer aid
Ere long consoled him.   Beauteous as the dawn
Next morn two shepherd boys seeking a lamb
Came on the sick man in his forest nook ;
Long time they gazed on him compassionate ;
With voice benign and tendance angel-like
Onward into his confidence they crept ;
His lips with milk, the purest, they refreshed ;
They placed the dewy wood flowers in his hand ;
They sang him ballads old, not battle-songs,
Too loud such songs they deemed, but Fairy lore,
Or tale of lovers fleeing tyrant's rage :
Among the last unwittingly they sang
'Cuchullain's Wooing ;' how the youth had found
Eimer, the loveliest lady of the land
Within her bowery pleasaunce, girt with maids
Harping, or broidering fair in scarf deep-dyed
Blossom or insect : how he sued ; and how
She answered ; 'Woo my sister : woo not me !'
How, glorying in her loveliness, her sire
Had sworn no chief should ever call her wife
Who won her not by valour ; how that youth
Had scaled his rock and slain his guards and forth
Led her by hand, a downward-looking bride,

Majestic, unconsenting, undismayed,
But likewise unreluctant. As they sang
Above that suffering face there passed a smile ;
And where that smile had lain there crept a tear ;
And in few minutes more asleep he sank
Who had not slept nine days.

                    Swiftly meanwhile
On marched the host confederate : bootless speed ;
Since ever one day's progress by the next
Was cancelled ; tortuous mind made tortuous course
Now bent awry to capture spoil, anon
To avenge some private wrong. Fergus the while
Inly with fury raged ; for still his thought
Was 'Eman—Vengeance.' Meave, to calm his wrath,
Albeit debate she scorned, a council called
And made demand, 'To Eman speed we, Kings,
With central wound striking at Uladh's heart,
Or wind, as now, at random through the realm,
With havoc huge, and plunder?'

                        Rose a chief
Aulnau, the son of Magach, one whose pride
Was not in war-deeds but in crafty brain,
And thus made answer. 'March to Eman ! Queen !
Not difficult the emprise ; but whose the gain ?
Eman to burn, what were it but to sow
The sanguine seed of endless wars to come ?

The Uladh chiefs live scattered.   Eman's fall
Touches not them.   Their strength ere long revived
Southward in search of vengeance they will rush :
Slay them yet weakling !   Slay them ere they wake !
Slay them in mountain hold and forest lair
In vale and glen : slay each apart, half-armed ;
Easy the task ! '   Arose the Exiled King :
' " Easy the task ! " ' he cried ; ' that Daré learned !
Unarmed—alone—I saw the old man fall !
" Easy the task ! " '   Then brake upon him Alp
That ruled in far Iorras, speaking thus ;
' Fergus, we love our queen ; but love not thee !
Hostile to ours thy race : King Conor's fall
Thou seek'st ; not Uladh's.   Hear me, Queen of Men !
The siege of Eman means a three months' siege :
Be wary lest, ere yet that time is past
King Conor with his exiles makes a pact,
And they who now but rate thee drink thy blood :
Be wary likewise lest in half that time
Thy host melt from thee like a wreath of snow !
The Gael is restless ; lives on chance and change ;
The clan grows home-sick : victory in its grasp,
Pines for the babe unkissed, or field unreaped :
My counsel then is Aulnau's.   Like a flood
Wind devious through the land and strip it bare :
Till then let Eman be.'

Debate ere long,
For chiefs there were who loved the nobler war,
Passed on to raging storm.   Old friendships died ;
And from the dust of ages injuries old
Leaped up like warriors armed.   In Fergus wrath
Gave way to scorn : with haughty port he spake,
A man majestical yet mirthful too.

   'Great Lords and Kings—since Kings ye claim to be—
King-vassals, world-renowned for mutual hate,
Alone of men I censure not your strifes,
Knowing their cause.   The very air you breathe,
The founts whereof you drink, the soil you tread,
Are all impregnate with a sacred rage ;
And false alike to usage, country, blood,
Were he among you who, for three hours' space,
Discerned 'twixt friend and foeman.   Lords and Kings,
Attend a legend from your annals old,
A laughing picture of man's life this day.
In Erin's earlier age there reigned two kings :
Each had a swineherd who, through magic power,
Assumed what form he would of shapes that live
In heaven, or earth, or sea.   Friendship eterne
They pledged ; then strove ten years, with hosts allied
So huge that none remained to till the land.
At last the vanquished westward creaked, a crane :
A crane, the victor chased him.   Twenty years

High up they fought ; to each side Erin's birds
Flocking in clans, the factions of the heavens.
Those twenty years run out, the vanquished crane
Dropp'd on a stream and straight to salmon changed ;
Instant his foe, to salmon turned not less,
From stream to sea pursued him.   Far and wide
All scaly shapes that buffet Erin's waves
From sprat and minnow up to shark and whale
Beat up in finny squadrons.   Forty years
With deepening rage they fought, till round the isle
Main ocean boiled, and from her ships black-ribbed
Melted the tar, and mist was over all.
Next changed those salmons twain to dragon-flies :
But while they sat in hate on neighbouring pools
A dun cow and a red cow drank them up
Unwittingly.   From them two bull-calves sprang
That, grown, with battle thunders dinned the realm
For eighty years !   How say ye, Lords ?   From these
Come not the Bulls that shake this day our land,
Fionbannagh, and the Donn ?   For them we fight,
And in their honour hold, on peaceful days,
Like them our roaring synods ! '

       Fiercely and long
The unwise council strove ; and Meave, who feared
Far more the petulance of her lesser kings
Than that great exile's loftier wrath, resumed

Next morn her march erratic.   On she passed,
The Dal Araidhé forests on her right,
Northward to Moira's plain and Clannaboy ;
And through the Glynns of Ardes glimpsed remote
Alba's blue hills.   Dalríad fastnesses
She burned with fire, and seized full many a herd
On banks of Bann ; then westward turned, and kenned
The grass-green glitter soon of far Lough Foyle,
And where the winding river-sea divides
Fanad from Inishowen's cliffs forlorn.
Aileach she passed, more late the seat of kings ;
And, southward next, that lake whose lonely isle
Descends, through caves, to Spirit-worlds unknown.
Thus Meave a circle traced round Uladh's realm,
And heard the murmur of its three great seas,
Yet nothing wrought of perdurable fame.
Conor, meantime, round Eman ranged his hosts
There flocking night and day.   ' I march not hence '
He said, ' till Uladh's wound is wholly healed ;—
Fergus I deem the sage of battle-fields,
Though fool in all beside.'
                              But sloth and fear
In manly hearts at worst rare visitants,
Leave them betimes, like vermin caught by chance
That quit ere long the clean.   O'er Uladh's breadth
Daily some chief, or fragment of a clan

Long chilled by rumour of Cuchullain slain,
Despite King Conor's hest assailed the queen
Marching, though late, on Eman.   First of these
Was Ketherne.   Hewing oaks on Fuad's crest
He marked her host, and rushed, a naked man
From waist to head, his axe within his hand,
In fury on it.   Late that eve his kernes
Forth from the battle tore him bleeding fast
From fifty wounds.   That night physicians five
Were bending o'er his bed : the eldest spake ;
'Ketherne, thou son of Fintan, thou must die !'
Then Ketherne raised himself and with one blow
Smote him upon his forehead that he died.
In turn the second,—'Ketherne, thou must die :'
And Ketherne slew him.   Feebler-toned the third
Whispered, ' The man must die ; ' and died himself ;
Likewise the fourth.   Old Ithal was the fifth,
A son of Alba.   He with stealthy foot
Stepping o'er corpses of his brethren slain,
Made keen-eyed inquest of the wounds ; then spake :
'Of these the least is dangerous : fatal none :
Two cures for such there be, diverse in kind ;
Ketherne, thou son of Fintan, make thy choice !
The first is slow but certain : where thou liest
Full three months thou must lie ; then rise restored :
The second is immediate : strength divine

It pours like light into a warrior's veins ;
Then dies its virtue, and the warrior dies !'
Ketherne laughed loud : 'My choice is quickly made—
Three months bed-ridden, or one vengeance day
Joyous and glorious !   Leech ! I rather choose
With mine own hand to avenge eretime my death
Than trust that task to others !'   At his word
Ithal prepared a wonder-working bath
Strewn with strange herbs, and bathed therein the man,
Then bade him drink of some elixir bright
Drawn from the sun.   As one refreshed by sleep
He rose : he clomb his war-car ; sought the foe ;
Threescore he slew, their best.   At last the strength
Ceased from his arm ; and opened once again
His wounds late closed ; and back he sank, and died.
  Such hindrances, and every day had such,
Likewise huge herds and cumber of her spoil
Slackened the march of Meave.   Full many a chief
Perished in bootless fight ; full many an eye
Turned on her, malcontent.   But trial worse
Had found her through her daughter, Finobar.
Without an hour's misgiving or remorse
In beauty's pride not less than patriot zeal—
Wilier she was than Meave, and haughtier far—
Champion on champion she had sent to doom
Beside that fatal Ford.   Ferdia most

Had tasked the sorceress, for in him alone
Vanity kept no place.   She watched the fight
No pallor on her fruit-like cheek, no cloud
Dimming her star-like eyes.   Without a sigh
She saw the Firbolg, last of all his race,
Fall on the soil once theirs.   Even then she knew not
The inevitable shaft had pierced whate'er
Of woman heart was hers.   The strong man's death
Lifted that veil his victory ne'er had raised :
Standing mid others she beheld him dead :
Thenceforth that deep-toned voice, that mournful front,
Those stern yet stately ways, so great and plain,
Haunted her memory.   Oft with sudden spasm
She strove to shake that viper from her breast
Which sucked its life-blood.   ' I, the Princess, love !
And love a Firbolg ! '   She had never loved :
Self-love, sole regent of the unloving heart,
Had barred it 'gainst all other tenderer loves :
In vain the island chiefs had wooed and sued :
She spurned them each and all.

                          Of these the last
Was Rochad, and the proudest, in the North
A vassal prince of Conor's, oft his foe :
The passion she had kindled she had scorned :
Rochad had vowed revenge.

In wonder Meave
Noted the weary lids, the vanishing bloom,
The abrupt accost, though haught yet unassured ;
The movements to mechanic changed, the mind
Still strong, yet widowed of its flexile strength ;
These things she saw ; their cause she ne'er divined :
Love for the living Meave could understand :
For her the dead was dead.   To Finobar
The one thing yet remaining was her pride :
Questioned, her answer ever was the same,
' Onward, to Eman ! '
           Nearer it each day
They drew.   One evening through the sunset mist
A camp, high-seated on a bosky hill,
Shone out, fire-fringed : aloof it stood as one
That halts 'twixt war and peace.   Ere long they learned
Rochad that site had chos'n, with Uladh's King
Friendly but half, thence slow to prop his cause.
Then spake the queen ; ' The hand of yonder chief
Sustains our battle's balance.   If his host,
Now dubious, joins the bands that vex our flank
No choice remains but this, a homeward course
Or, if a march to Eman, then the loss
Of half our hard-earned spoil and hate thenceforth
Of all our vassal kings.'   Forth flashed the eyes

Of Finobar—it was their latest flash—
She answered thus ; 'The sequel leave to me !
He loved me, Rochad, once : ere sets yon moon
I bring you tamed the lion of yon hills,
Aye, in a silken leash !'
　　　　　　　　Rochad far off
Beheld her coming ; marked it with a smile ;
Welcomed her gaily ; led her to the feast ;
Thence to his tent wherein was none beside.
There put she forth whatever subtlest art
In seeming-simple innocence disguised
Imagines of persuasive, whatsoe'er
Delicatest craft of female witcheries
Potent for man's destruction can devise,
To bend that warrior's will.　The winter beam
Thaws not the polar ice : o'er Rochad's soul
So passed the syren's pleadings.　Pleased not less
To stand implored, he dallied with her suit
Destined, and this he knew, to end in shame.
She, self-deceived, inly made vow ; 'This tent
I leave not, save victorious.'
　　　　　　　　Hours went by :
She noted not their flight.　Once more with skill
Plastic as wind in woods, a measured strength
Varying as minstrel's hand that grazes now
Now sweeps the tenderer or the deeper strings,

To all the passions of the heart of man
Glory, Ambition, Love, Revenge, she tuned
The modulations of her passionate strain ;
While half the richness theirs aforetime throbbed
Again in those sad accents, half their light—
For oft from out the present shines a past
Long dead—returned to eyes that, seen of none,
Had wept away their splendours. Calm he sat,
Sternly quiescent. Sudden on her broke
The fatal truth. She saw her power was gone ;
And all that posthumous life late hers sank back
In embers lost and ashes. On the West
Rested her gaze. A cloud of raven black,
Its veil for half that night, had drifted by,
And o'er that distant gleam, her mother's camp,
Slowly the moon descended. Finobar
That hour recalled her boast ; ' Ere sets yon moon
I bring you tamed the lion of yon hills,
Aye, in a silken leash ! '
                              The Orient soon
Whitened with early dawn. Forlorn it lay
On hill and heath and plain and distant mere,
Forlorner on the haggard face—for oft
A face, still fair, in anguish antedates
Its future—of that woman as she knelt,
She knelt at last, low on that threshold low.

Then came the hour of Rochad's great revenge :
Then first he answered plainly ; ' Finobar !
One day I knew you not : I know you now :
Your spells are null when once their trick is learned :
Likewise your face has lost its earlier charm.
Back to your mother !   Say, ere sets yon sun
I join the king my master, from his gate
Repel with scorn the invader.'   Forth he passed
Without farewell.   A clarion broke ere long
Her trance : adown the slope she saw his host
Winding t'ward Eman.

            From a burning couch
She rose next eve ; and, strong with fever's strength,
Paced swiftly by that sunset-crimsoned stream
Which cut the camp in twain.   Anon she marked
In all who met her, change inexplicable,
Strange eyes, strange faces, strange embarrassed ways :
Sadly compassionate that change in some :
In others questioning glance and meaning smile
Hinted at things that through her flaming heart
Passed like a sword of ice.   Whisperings not less
There were, but these she heard not ; 'What !   All
    night !
From eve to morn with Rochad in his tent !—
The men she fed on hopes she sent to death
Beside the Ford.   Well ! pride must have its fall !

Rochad is joined with Conor !'   Slanders worse
Some chiefs whom most her haughtiness had galled
Ventured, vain-glorious.   Late one eve the truth
Sprang like a tigress on her.   In his tent
She heard her father with her mother speak ;
'She yet may wear the crown : her maiden fame
Is lost forever !'

                Three hours ere her death
Thus to her mother spake that sentenced one ;
'Noise it among the host that grief for those
Her countrymen—the Gael—who, near the Ford—
Ere yet that Firbolg shared the common fate,
Fell by Cuchullain, snapped her thread of life.
Bear on your march my body :—raise the cairn
On the first hill that kens Emania's towers.'

   So spake she ; and the queen obeyed her hest :
She flung that rumour forth ; and all who heard,
Heart-stricken now, believed it.   But on Meave
A piercing sadness fell ; and by her bed
Orloff her buried son stood up, and spake ;
'Home to thy native realm, and Cruachan !
Not less a battle waits thee great and dread
'Twixt Gairig and Ilgairig.'   One day's march
Eastward still marched she ; then upon a hill,
The first whose summit looked on Eman's towers,
Interred the all-beauteous one with Pagan dirge,

And o'er her piled the cairn.   Southward, next morn
She turned, and crossed the Ford.   Fulfilled was thus
Cuchullain's word, breathed o'er Ferdia dead,
' Finobar snared thee.   Finobar shall die.'
    But many a century later Uladh's sons
Rose up and said ; ' Great scorn it is and wrong
Yon stranger's grave should gaze on Eman's towers : '
Then bore they forth those relics once so fair
With funeral rites revered and Pagan dirge,
And laid them by the loud-resounding sea,
And o'er them raised a cairn : and, age on age,
As sighed the sea-wind past it shepherds said
' It whispers soft that sad word, Finobar ! '

FRAGMENT V.

QUEEN MEAVE'S RETREAT.

ARGUMENT.

QUEEN MEAVE, having reached the sacred plain of Uta, sacrilegiously encamps thereon. A Druid denounces the late war as unrighteous, while Fergus contemns it as ineffectual; and immediately afterwards the Mor Reega manifests herself to the host. Next evening, while division of the spoil is being made, Meave is ware of the advance of King Conor; and Ailill transfers the supreme command to Fergus, who prepares for the attack. The battle is gloriously won by Fergus. That night Meave is warned by signs and omens; and Cuchullain, weak from his wounds, arrives in the Ulidian camp. From midnight to near sunset the next day he lies in a trance, during which fair spirits minister to him again his lost strength; and there is shown to him a vision of some mystic greatness reserved for Erin, yet of an order which he cannot understand. When the second battle is well nigh lost Cuchullain wakes; and Meave is driven in utter overthrow across the Shannon.

At last the war had whirled its giddy round ;
And Meave, well nigh returned, the Shenan [1] near
Beside Ath-Luain streaming in its might,
Decreed to make division of her spoil

[1] The Shannon.

Ere yet she crossed it.   In the West the sun
Was sinking ; in the East the moon uprose ;
While camped her host on Uta's sacred plain
Betwixt the double glories.   Far away
Immeasurably glittered the pastures green
Illumed with million flowers.   Nor spade, nor plough
Till then that virgin region had profaned ;
Nor sound, save Shenan's murmur, stirred therein.
There stood the Tomb Heroic.   Beams and showers
Alone might pierce that soil sabbatical;
Such reverence held the spot.   Now all was changed ;
Ill choice ; if chance, ill-omened.   Neighing steeds
Dinned the still air ; while here at times was heard
Whistling of him that fixed his tent, and there
Wood-cleaving axe or feaster's laugh mistimed.
Higher and higher rose the moon full-orbed,
Mirrored in pool and stream.   At intervals
Half lost in bard-song near or shout remote,
The slender wailing of some captive maid
Rang out and died.

　　　　　　　The royal tent was set
High on a grassy platform.   Meave that night
The first time since the death of Finobar
Was cheerful of aspéct ; and, banquet o'er,
Rising her warriors she addressed with vaunt
Beseeming not a queen.   'A year,' she said,

' Is past since northward to the war we marched :
Then forth she loosed the sheets and spread the sails
And bounded on the waves of proud discourse
Recounting all her triumphs ; first, her wrong ;
Lastly, the cause of war, Cuailgné's Donn
Chief captive mid her captives ! Here her voice
Rang loudest, and her eyes their fiercest beamed.
Rapturous response succeeded ; one alone,
A Druid old, dissentient. Thus he spake,
Not rising, to that throng of courtiers crowned :
' Ill doctrine have ye praised this evening, kings,
Unwise, to Erin's realms unprofitable,
Extolling war not based on righteous cause
Nor righteous ends ensuing. Kings and queen,
The end of war is retribution just
For deeds unjust ; ill cure for greater ill :
Wars there must be ; and woman-mouthed were he
Who railed against them :—aye, but demon-mouthed
The man that boasts of war-dishonouring wars
Opprobrious, spiteful, predatory, base.
Sirs, how began this feud ? It rose from jest !
And what its close ? A sacred site profaned,
Inviolate till this day ! ' The warriors frowned ;
Yet all men feared the Druid beard and rod :
They stood in silence.
                            Fergus rose, and spake :

'Sirs, I have heard a war this day extolled,
A war this day denounced.   On battle-field
Men say that I was born ; on battle-fields
Have lived from youth to age.   What thing war is
I ought to know.   Yet, sirs, these wearied eyes
Rolled many a day around from East to West
Still seeking war, and found it not : they saw
Six hundred men successive by the hand
Of one man slain, Cuchullain ; saw the torch
Hurl the red smoke-cloud o'er a thousand homes :
They saw a war-dance circle Uladh's coasts ;
They saw the ravished flock, and ravished herd,
The captive throng lance-goaded on its way,
Swine-herd and shepherd, hoary head, and maid
Beaming and basking in the healthful glow
Of youthful beauty.   Sirs, they saw more late,
But saw from distance, Eman's walls high-towered :
This, this they saw not ; warriors, warrior-ruled,
Marching against them !   Mountebanks of war
They saw ; not warriors !'

                Plainly Fergus spake :
Not otherwise than plainly could he speak,
A man to Truth predestined ; since his birth
By courage sealed to Truth.   The legend saith
That down before him on his natal morn
All Erin's fays and sprites from river or rill

Their tributes laid.   But, mightier far than they,
A wingèd goddess ran from sea to sea,
The island's breadth, to hail him !   As she sped,
The path before her, prone till then and low,
Rising ran out a craggy ridge sublime,
The same that for a hundred miles this day
Divides the realm.   That highway lofty and straight
Foreshowed that ne'er in tortuous ways or base
Should walk that infant.

                    Raging, from their seats
The kings and chieftains leaped.   A hundred swords
Flashed from their sheaths, and from a hundred mouths
One sentence issued—' Death !'   By twos and threes
A score of stragglers from the exiles' band
Closed up behind him.   Cormac Conlinglas
Beside him stood, sword drawn.

                    Again he spake ;
' Queen, till that day of shame was battle none,
Nor on that day ; nor since !   But on that day
Beside your daughter's cairn—more royal far
Though fortunate less was she—we two conversed :
I said ; " Without one blow you think to pass
Eman, that cast me forth !   Without one blow
To cross your Shenan, reach your Cruachan,
There make your terms secure, the spoil retained,
The exiles sent to judgment !   Note you, Queen,

Those horsemen three a mile on yonder road ?
My heralds they !   The hour your flight begins
They speed to Eman."

                              ' You retreated.   They
Rode on to Conor.   To that chief of foes
I wrote ; " Advance !   The queen retreats : make speed :
She shall not 'scape the battle.   Know besides
That battle of earth's battles till this hour
Shall prove the bloodiest.   In it, sword to sword
We two shall meet ; one die." '

                              In measureless scorn
Then turned he to the kings, continuing thus ;
' What mean those clamours and those swords half
     drawn
Which draw ye dare not ?   Petty, titular kings !
The shadow of that royalty once mine
Dwarfs you to pygmies by comparison !
I heard a cry of " Treason ! "   Let them lift
Their hands who raised it !   Kinglings mutinous,
Princes seditious, ye the traitors are !
And on the nod of him whom ye traduce,
Your pageant crowns sit trembling.   Ere three days
Uladh is on you !   I shall stand that hour
Your King Elect ; not Ailill's choice, but yours ;
The Battle-King ; for well ye know that I,
None else, have skill to range the battle-field,

And roll the thunders forth of genuine war.
Till that hour, silence, kings !'
                           Silence they kept,
Long silence.   Then far off, as though from depths
By thought untraversable of cloudless skies,
Such sound was heard as reaches ships at sea
When, launched on airy voyage though still remote,
Nation of ocean-crossing birds begins
To obscure the serene heaven.   That sound drew near :
From every tent the revellers rushed.   Then lo !
That portent seen alone in fateful times,
The dread Mor Reega !   Terrible as Fate
The goddess of the battles high o'er head
Sailed on full-panoplied, in hue as when
On Alpine snows, their sunset glories gone,
Night's winding-sheet descends.   Upon her casque
And spear beyond it pointing glared the moon,
And on a face like hers that froze of old
The gazers into stone.   As on she sailed
On that huge army coldness fell of death :
Yea, some there died.   Next morning, from that spot
Northward to Eman lay a branded track :
Straight as a lance still stretched it, league on league ;
A bar of winter black through harvest fields,
A bridge of ice spanning the rippling waves ;
A pledge that men had dreamed not.

                                        In those days
Foreboding soon, like sorrow, passed away :
Ailill next morning counselled ; ' Ere the night
Cross we the Shenan.   If the Red Branch comes
Fight we on Ai's plain ! '   But Meave replied
' Not so ; I fly not !   One day here we rest :
Our kings await their spoil.'

                              From morn to eve
That spoil's partition lasted ; first, huge herds ;
Flocks snowy-white through water-weeds and grass
Followed, hound-driven.   War-horses few were there,
But many from the plough : with these, in crowds
Poor hinds, and swine-herds, maidens skilled in works
That knew to spin the flax or mix the dye
Or card the wool.   Next followed wild-eyed boys
Bound each to each.   No tear they shed, but scowled
Defiance on their lords and war-songs sang
Of Uladh and her vengeance.   King and chief
Scanned each his prize with careless-seeming eye;
Yet oft their followers strove, while onward paced
The royal arbiters with wands high held,
Ruling the wrangling crew.

                              Upon a mound
Meantime the royal throne was set, a throng
Of warriors round it.   Many a mirthful chance
Provoked their laughter : loudest laughed the queen ;

But when she spake she waited not reply.
Without a bound to east and west and south
The prospect spread.   Her eye was on the north :—
Not distant stood two hills : she asked their names :
Her great eyes darkened when the answer came
Of Gairig and Ilgairig.

               'Twixt these twain,
Shone out, distincter as the sun declined,
Long northern ranges.   Fergus marked her eye
That moved not from them, smiled, and made demand,
'What find'st thou in our mountain ridges, Queen,
That merits gaze so fixed?'   Then she ; 'I note
Girdling their slopes a mist feathery and soft,
As though of snow-flakes wov'n : above it peaks
Shoot up, like isles cloud-hid.   Within that mist
I see strange lights that cross like shooting stars ;
Cross and re-cross, quick-bickering.'   With a smile
That deepened, Fergus questioned once again :
'Make large thine eyes and tell me what thou seest !'   ·
Then Meave ; 'Through all that mist is movement
     strange,
The agitation of some wondrous life,
And t'wards us on it rolleth.'   Fergus next ;
'Thine eyes see well !   If others saw like thee
Their tongues would clang less loudly.   Hear'st thou
     nought?'

The queen made answer ; ' Many a sea I hear
That breaks on many a shore.'

                           Then Fergus cried
' Thou seest my Uladh coming, and the way
And fashion of the advent of her war !
For know, great Queen, even now the Red Branch
      Knights
Car-borne descend yon slopes !   That mist thou saw'st
What is it but the tempest of their march,
The dust flung upwards and the sweat exhaled
And visible breath of warrior and of horse
That breathes the northwind and the sunny glare ?
What else the snow-flakes which thou saw'st but foam
Dashed from the horses' bits ?   Thy bickering stars,
What else but flaming cars and fiery helms
This way and that way passing ?   What thy peaks
Crowning that mist, but Uladh's hills remote
That send her children to avenge her wrong ?
And what that thunder sound of many seas
But music of their coming ?   Well for thee
If o'er them sail not, veiled from mortal eyes,
That dread Mor Reega ! '

                        Reddened as he spake
Meave's cheek late pale ; yet careless she replied ;
' I see her not, therefore believe her not,
And breathe securely since that gleam far off

Is human, not demoniac or divine ;
For never feared I yet the arm of man :
Cuchullain dead, I hold at nought the rest.'
Thus Meave : but all the kings and chiefs arose
Clamouring to her and Ailill ; ' Lo, 'tis come !
All Uladh, and a battle such as ne'er
Shook the foundations of this kingly isle !
Now therefore bid him rule thy host, the man
That knows to rule ! ' 'Twixt passions twain at war
Meave silent stood. Ailill to Fergus turned
And spake ; ' Be thou henceforth our Battle-King:'
Thus spake he ; then, releasing from his belt
The sword usurped of Fergus, added thus ;
' Receive once more thy sword ! in mirth erewhile
I made it mine : the virtue in that blade
Hath kept me till this hour.' Fergus replied ;
' I take mine own : but one month past, this sword
Had cut the cancer out of Uladh's breast,
And made thy throne a praise on earth for aye !
I take mine own, on thee a sword bestowing
That best becomes thee. Waiting long this hour
For thee I kept it.' Proudly Ailill clasped
Its glittering hilt : Fergus drew back the sheath ;
And lo, a wooden sword, for babes a toy !
The concourse laughed ; the loudest Meave : though
    wroth

Ailill a little whiffling laugh essayed
With sidelong face.

        Then Fergus in the soil
Planting his sword upright before it knelt,
And spake ; 'O thou my sovereignty, my sword,
In many a battle, yet in none unjust,
So many a year my glory and my mate !
Mine art thou, mine once more !   In all this host
Who shall henceforth reproach me ? '

                 To his task
The strong one sped, and change was over all :
Again the voice of discipline was heard :
None drank in booths ; none rushed abroad ; with sloth
Fierceness had vanished.   Followers of the camp
Alone were left in charge of flocks and herds :
The clansmen to their duties were restored,
The clans in order ranged.   He delved a trench
Barring from Uta's plain the advancing foe,
And bridges o'er it flung, that so his host
Permission given, and not till then, might strike
Forth pouring torrent-like at Uladh's heart :
Pits too he dug bristling with stakes sod-hid.
He gave command like one that, born to power,
With courteous might scarce conscious puts it forth :
He spake the word : all heard him : all obeyed
Magnanimous to feel when majesty

Authentic stood before them.   Duty done
Engendered strenuous joy, and strength, and hope :
Thus through the mass the spirit of one man
Triumphed, and ruling, raised it : on each face
His corporal semblance lived—light hearted might,
Deliberate resolve.
                         The moonlight hours
Shone brightly on their labours.   Six had sped
Ere Fergus sought the royal tent where sat
Revellers right ill at ease.   As in he passed,
The concourse, Meave herself and Ailill, rose,
And did him regal honours.   Of his toils
Nought spake he ; but their hearts who saw him swelled
And many marvelled why they late were sad :
Again the laugh ; again the tale ; the song—
Then came a change.   A gradual sound was heard,
Yet what and whence they knew not.   It increased ;
It swelled ere long, voluminous ; grating next ;
Then dreadful like the splitting of a world
Whose strong foundations crumble.   Forth they passed
Through hurrying clouds the moon rushed madly on,
Now dim, now fiercely glaring.   From the north
In terror sped the forest beasts and dashed
Wild through the camp while panic fell on all.
The sole man unastonished, Fergus spake :
'Sirs, late ye learn our warfare !   As the spring,

When the first spray catches the amorous red,
Her song-bird sends, herald and harbinger,
So Uladh sends before her onward steps
Her shrill-voiced vanguard : men of might are they,
Hewers of war-ways for her battle cars
Advancing through the forests.   First ye heard
Their axes only ; last, the falling trees :—
What, Sirs, ye look like men ill-pleased !   Well, well !
Not all delight in music.   Sirs, good-night !
When breaks the dawn be stirring.'

       In the camp
Few slept that night.   Vanished the moon in cloud :
Then shone the watch-fires on the northern hills
Like stars.

     Next morn the Uladh host down swarmed
Betwixt those neighbouring hills and round their base
Far spread as flood that, widening on its way,
Changes the heights to islands.   Countless wrongs
And shame at all that long inglorious trance,
Roused wrath to madness ; from them far they flung
Encumbering arms, and, bare from scalp to waist,
Worked on with brandished battle-axe.   Three hours
That trench withstood them.   Kelkar ruled their left,
Their right great Conal Carnach, while the king
Marshalled their centre.   There the strongest bridge,
Tower-guarded, longest held their host at bay ;

Longer had held it, save that from his place
Fergus, the hour foreseen arrived, gave word
' Fling wide the gates ! '   In rushed they ; but to meet
A foe unwasted yet.   The Red Branch Knights
Surpassed their old renown.   In fresher strength
The host confederate met them.   Meave herself
With downward mace three champions slew that day,
Him last, that felon son of faithful sire,
Buini, the Ruthless Red, who, breaking pledge,
Betrayed the sons of Usnach for a bribe :
His father's prophecy the Accursed fulfilled
Slain by a woman's hand.   Fergus, at last
Forth launched upon his native element,
Raced o'er the battle billows like a bark
When tempests stretch its canvass.   Chief on chief
Went down before that sword that still, men sware,
With sweep that widened like a rainbow's arch
Ran from his hand and harvests reaped of death.
O'er-spent, not scared, that Northern host gave way
Sudden from east to west.   It broke and fled.
    Alone unvanquished Conor Conchobar
Maintained his place.   He rallied twice and thrice
The fugitives ; thrice turned them on the foe ;
Then stabbed them flying.   Last upon the bridge
He stood and sole.   There met him face to face
The sole of foes his equal.   Dreadful gaze

Long fixed they, each on other ; Fergus spake :
' Is this indeed that king who filched that realm
Not his, then shamed it by a bloodier fraud ;
Who brake his pledge ; who murdered Usnach's sons ;
Who drave from Uladh, Uladh's rightful king ;—
And comes he at my hand to meet his doom ?
Just Gods, I thank you !' With a haughtier mien,
Yet kingly less, King Conchobar replied :
' 'Thou know'st me ; and 'tis well ! That king am I
Who, less than thou by lineage, but in mind
Loftier, attained that crown thou could'st not keep ;
That king, who, breaking through a jesting pact
As eagles through a mist, by doom deserved
Requited rebels proved. That king am I
Who, when with traitors thou true pact hadst made,
Forth hurled thee naked to the wild wolf's lair :
That was the worst I wished thee : worse by far
If aught of kingly once was thine thou found'st—
Beneath a hostile roof the beggar's dole
Gorged on a golden platter, and the hand
Protectress, of a woman !'
                           Long that fight
Watched by two hosts in speechless stupor held,
Direful and long ! Equal in might those twain,
Equal in craft of war. The kinglier soul
Conferred alone the victory. Fergus raised

The unvanquishable sword so late restored :
It fell in thunder : with it fell the king,
Fell to his knees, a bleeding mass, and blind :
Again that sword was raised : a moment more
Had ended all : then leaped to Fergus' feet,
His knees enclasping, Cormac Conlinglas
King Conor's son.   He spake these words alone :
' My father !—Spare him !'   Fergus ne'er had scorned
A look like his that hour.   He turned : he spake ;
' Take hence that reptile :—holy is this plain !
A true king here was buried !'   Conor's kernes
Lifted him to his war-car.   Slowly it moved ;
For Death was in the wheels thereof ; and Death
Stood at its door.

                That night in Uladh's camp
Was silence strange and dread.   By dying men
Sat men sore wounded.   Scornful of their foe
And burning for revenge, the North had spurned
Science of war, their boast, and left, death-strewn,
Full half their host.   Between their tents and Meave's
All that long night the buriers of the dead
Groped their sad way with red, earth-grazing torch,
Turning the white face up in search of friend,
Brother, or son.   But in the tent of Meave
Triumph ruled all : a hundred spake at once
Each man his deeds recounting.   Far apart

Sat Fergus ; on his brow alone was shade :
The deed was needful ; but his country's blood
Gladdened not him.   Of those that marked him, some
Had reverence for his sadness : lesser souls
That long had hated, loathed the man that hour.
Sudden the din surceased.   Far other sound
Quelled it : from Uladh's sorrowing camp it swelled,
A jubilant cry soaring from earth to heaven !
Then flashed the eyes of Fergus, and he cried ;
'Cuchullain lives !   That sound is Uladh's shout
What time the host he enters ! '   With a brow
Gloomy as night the queen replied ; ' 'Tis false !
We know that in the forest, months gone by
Cuchullain perished ! '   Silent long they stood ;
Listening.   At last rang out far different note
As piteous as the first was full of joy,
A funeral *keen* world-wide.   Then cried the queen,
'Cuchullain lived !   Cuchullain lives no more !
Wounded and weak he came to aid his own :
Too great such effort for a wasted frame :
That was Cuchullain's death-dirge ! '   Fierce she stood :
Glorying she spake, and with attendance passed
Forth from the hall of banquet to her tent :
But as she passed she heard at either side
She and her ladies with her, trembling heard
The rushing of a panic-stricken host

Invisible, though now the dawn was grey,
A host t'ward Shenan flying !   High o'er head
A dulcet strain, unutterably sad,
When ceased that phantom rush of fugitive feet,
Drifted far northward.   Then the queen was ware
These were her country's gods that left her host.
The legend adds that in her tent that hour
Faythleen, the witch, she saw, who sat and wove
A mystic web and sang a mystic song,
Seen but by her :—and, later, o'er her bed
Men say that Orloff bent, her buried son,
And spake ; 'This day the battle shall be fought
Of Gairig and Ilgairig.'
                              He meanwhile,
The lord of all the battles, where was he,
Cuchullain ?   Many a weary day and week
Within his loved Murthemné's woods he lay,
Sore-wounded man nigh death.   Those shepherd
      youths
Tended him still, or sang beside his bed ;
And ofttimes o'er his face the tears of Leagh
In passionate gust descended.   But the might
Unholy of the clan of Cailitin
That nightly hung above him like a cloud
Began to wither when that mist accursed
Drifted from Uladh's borders.   On the breast

Pellucid, likewise, of Murthemné's streams
Benignant spirits scattered flowers and herbs
With healing virtue dowered.   He, morn and eve
In those clear currents laid, renewed his youth ;
And, pure as infant's, came again that flesh
Where festered late his wounds.   At last, revived,
He passed, car-borne to Eman, north.   The fields
Devastated, and wail from foodless glens
Filled him as on he sped with wrathful strength :
Next, tidings came of Conor's southward march :
Exultingly he followed.   On that night
Of overthrow he reached the royal camp :
Far off they kenned his car, and raised that shout
Heard never save for him.   When near he drew
Way-worn, and wearied, and around him gazed,
And saw that sight, and thought, ' too late ; too late ! '
His cheek upon the shoulder sank of Leagh,
And all men deemed him dead.   Then rose that wail
To Meave auspicious sound.

                There are who deem
Cuchullain's tent that night was near the Well
Where, purer far, more late the royal maids
Fedelm and Ethna met that saint who gave
To God the isle of Fate.   Blessing then too
That Well diffused, they say ; for from its brink
A runnel o'er the pebbles ran with sound

So sweetly tuned that on the warrior sank
Deep seal of peace divine.   The war-shouts near
To him thus harboured seemed but ocean's sighs
Round islands ever calm.   Then came, on winds
Fresher than earth's, divinities more high
He thought than those that late from elfin meres
Amid Murthemné's woods had dewed his face ;
And loftier songs were sung ; and balmier flowers
In holier fountains bathed were softlier pressed
On breast and brow ; while shone before his eyes
Visions more fair than lordliest battle-field,
Though what they meant he knew not nor divined—
High-towerèd temples cruciform that rose
Far-seen o'er wood and street ; and from their gates
Vestal procession issuing white, that wound
Through precincts low where only dwelt the poor,
The halt, the lame, the blind ; and song he heard
With spiritual pathos changing sense to soul,
' The end of all is peace.'   In silence slid
The constellations down the western sky ;
And endless seemed that night.
                              At break of day
Came Conal Carnach and the Red Branch Knights
To see the sick man's face.   Thereon the morn
Laughed, dewy-bright : and lo ! where long had lain
Pallor of death, now burned a healthful red :

Not less they dared not touch him ; since with him
Geisa it was if any broke his rest.
They left him, and the battle-storm began.
Warned by defeat Uladh had raised ere morn,
Fronting her camp, three bulwarks : at the first
And distant most, three hours the conflict raged.
It fell at last.   When rose the conquerors' shout
Leagh to Cuchullain crept, and touched him not,
Yet knelt and whispered, ' Heard you not that sound ? '
And thus Cuchullain answered still in trance ;
' I heard the runnels in Murthemné's woods
Snow-swoll'n in spring.'   Then Leagh stood up and
    mused
' The hue of health is on his face, and yet
Because he will not wake the land is shamed.'
Next round the second bulwark raged the war
Hour after hour : heroic deeds were done :
Heroic deaths were died : at last it fell :
Again and nearer rose the conquerors' shout :
Again with bolder foot and forehead flushed
Leagh to Cuchullain moved and touched him not
But, bending, murmured, ' Heard you not that sound ? '
And he, without awaking, answered thus ;
' I heard the birds in Eimer's pleasaunce sing
To greet our marriage morn.'   Then Leagh went forth
Groaning, and smote his hands, and wept aloud

'Because he will not wake the host must die!'
Around the loftiest bulwark and the last
Once more for hours the battle raged : it fell !
And louder thrice that shout went up.   The gaze
Of Leagh was on him fixed : he heard it not :
Slowly it died ; and as it died the wail
Came feebly forth from Uladh's host.   A change
Flashed o'er Cuchullain's face : like fire it shone :
Into his tent he sprang midway !   Then lo !
A marvel ! for the wounded man that slept
All day with bandages enswathed, up-towered
Full-armed for fight a champion spear in hand,
Work of some god !   Swift from his tent he strode :—
Without the hand of man there stood his car
And those immortal steeds pawing the air
With wonted battle-cry !   A moment more
And forward to Ilgairig's slope they dashed :
'Let but the armies see him,' inly mused
Leagh, 'and the work is done ! '
                                        Onward they sped ;
But not unnoted by that demon brood
That hate the works of justice.   From below
Writhing in torment of their rage they heaved
The grassy surface upward into waves
Now swelling, now descending.   Strong albeit
The immortal steeds staggered.   Cuchullain cried,

' What ! children of the tempest-wakened lakes
Saw ye till now no billows ?   Yours they are !
Exult ye in your native element,
And waft your lord to vengeance ! '   They obeyed :
They reached Ilgairig's summit.

On he sped
Mantled with sunset.   Terrible he shone !
Both armies saw him—knew him !   Onward yet ;
While from his golden arms and golden car
Lightnings went forth incessant.   In his van
Victory and Fear their pinions spread.   He reached
Ilgairig's southern verge : he reined his steeds :
High in his car he stood ; with level hand
Screening his eyes he scanned that battle-field,
His future course decreeing.

On and on
Adown that slope he flashed and o'er that plain.
Like zigzag sunshaft o'er the autumnal world ;
And ever where he came the host of Meave
Gave way before him.   On and ever on !
And now the nearest of those bulwarks three
He reached, and o'er its ruins swept, back driving
The conquerors late now conquered.   On and on !
And ever through that foe thick-packed he clave
A lane of doom and death.   Ere long was reached
The second rampart.   There it was he slew

The great ones of Clan Libna, and the clans
Guairé and Murdoc.   Fiery faces thronged
The air around him, and the voice of Gods
Made smooth his way triumphant.

On and on—
Nor ceased he ever hurling left and right
Destruction from his sling ; nor slackened sleet
Of javelins winged with fate.   That brazen urn
With death-stones heaped exhausted not its store,
Replenished ever as by hand unseen
Work of some God !   That brazen cirque, not less
Where stood his javelins ranged was never void ;
Work of some God !   The on-rolling wheels devoured
Those serried ranks ; the war-steeds trampled down :
Reached was that rampart furthest of the three ;
There in her war-car sat the queen ; in front
The Maineys seven were ranged : his sword forth flashed :
Four perished of the seven.   Then faced the queen
Westward, and fled amazed.

He marked her flight :
Eastward he turned.   As on he carved his course
Not now a lane alone of doom and death
But ever widening valleys ruin-strewn
Bore witness of his transit, for behind
Closed ever up Cuchullain's household clans
Murthemné's, and Cuailgné's.   Perished there

Q

The Ossorians, and the Olnemacian chiefs,
And many a champion famed from Slaney's bank
To Lee and Laune, from Caiseal's crested rock
To Beara's strand.   Who died not, fled and left
Yet ampler 'twixt the bristling flanks of war
That vacant space ; and as the dolphin oft
Raptured by gladness of clear summer seas
While flames the noon on purple billows, swims
All round and round some ship full-sailed, so he
Circled on foot at times that car wind-swift
Mocking its slowness ; then with airy bound
Once more within it beamed.   His boyhood's mirth
Returned upon him.   On the chariot's floor
He marked those brazen balls, the sport that time
Of men way-faring, snatched them up, tossed high
While yet careering round the blood-stained field,
Then caught them as they fell :—a glittering ring
They girt that glittering head.   Not less his eye
Watchful pursued the flying foe ; his hand
Brought down to earth the fleetest.

                              From the crests
Of those twinned hills down rushed the total strength
At last of Uladh.   Universal flight
Shook the vast field.   The bravest men and best
Caught by its current on were dragged like trees
The sport of winter flood.   Chieftain and king

Sought, each, his home. Meave, with a remnant small
Reached Shenan's bridgeless tide ; and there had fallen
Stretching to towered Ath-Luain helpless hands,
Save that Cuchullain, 'mid the narrower way
Standing with arms extended, terrible,
Abashed that host pursuing ; 'Stand ye back !
One day I shared her feast : she shall not die !
He spake, and set by Shenan's wave his shield.
Next morn the Ulidians where that shield had stood
In silence stern planted three pillar-stones,
White daughters of the tempest-beaten hills,
In Ogham graved, 'Vanquished by Uladh's sons
Here fled the invader, Meave.'

      Fergus alone
The Exile-King, and they, the Exile Band,
Fled not that day. Though few and bleeding fast
Fearless upon a cloudy crag they stood,
Phalanx prepared to die, prepared not less
Dearly to sell their lives, while past them streamed
That panic-stricken throng. The host pursuing
Looked up, yet swerved not from their course. Once more
Returning from the vengeance they looked up ;
Then passed in silence by.

      That eve, men say,
While slowly paced Cuchullain t'ward the camp,

Lamenting strains of Goddesses were heard,
For whatsoe'er was female loved the man,
If earthly female, with a human love,
If heavenly, with a love compassionate,
Lamenting strains that, ere his youth had passed,
That starry head must lie by Fate's decree
Amid the dust of death.   Cuchullain turned ;
Softly he answered ; ' Goddesses benign !
Why weep ye?   I was Uladh's Mastiff-Hound :
The mastiff lives not long.   What better lot
For him than this ;—the bandits chased, to die
Beside his master's gate?'

So ends the *Tain* :
Not less, in mirth or spleen, that legend old
Primeval battle-chaunt of Erin's race,
Adds yet a second close.
Cuchullain led
That host Ulidian home ; while Meave made oath
Northward to send, and range round Eman's walls
Her spoil, the war's sole triumph, countless flocks,
The herds milk-yielding of the large-eyed kine,
The horses, and the asses, and the goats,
The household stuffs, rich vests, and precious dyes
The hinds laborious, and the men age-bent,
And maidens skilled in work ; but, first, and chief

That sable Bull, the cause of all the war.
Fulfilled were all these pledges save the last ;
For Meave upon that fatal day, while hung
Doubtful the battle-scales, had given command
To lead the Donn to Cruachan.   Ill-pleased
He on his keepers turning slew a score,
Yet peaceful paced at last betwixt their ranks,
At each side fifty spears.   Next day, far south,
Forth rolled the roar of Ailill's Bull snow-white,
Fionbannah.   Bursting through his guard, the Donn
Rushed t'ward the sound.   Upon the midway plain
The rivals met.   All day that battle raged
While wood to wood thunder on thunder hurled,
And all the bulls of Erin sent reply.
Shepherds, through wood-skirts peering, saw the end,
The Donn, at sunset, rushing t'ward the north,
And, on his conqueror's back—their horns entwined—
Fionbannah dead !   All night that conqueror rushed
O'er hill and plain and prone morass.   When dawn
Looked coldly forth through mist along the meads
Far off he kenned a rock : that rock he deemed
A second bull : collecting all his might
Thereon he hurled his giant bulk, and died.

Northward thus marched from Cruachan the kings ;
Then back.   The Foray of Queen Meave thus far.

NOTES.

Page 9.   *He taught her all the Ogham Signs to read.*

The Ogham characters are a species of alphabet, or as some call them cypher, cut upon stones, or wooden staves.   They are found in many parts of Ireland ; and much has been written on them by the most learned Irish antiquarians of recent times, especially by Bishop Graves.

Page 38.   *By Geisa bound.*

These *Gesa*, or *Geisa*, often as trivial in character as they were rigidly enforced, have a large place in the legends of the Irish pre-Christian times.   Sometimes they applied to particular individuals alone : thus, in the case of Cuchullain, it was a *Gesa* that no one should wake him out of his sleep.   Sometimes they were self-imposed : thus Fergus Mac Roy and Cuchullain also, had bound themselves in youth never to refuse an invitation to the feast of a good man, however humble.   The most remarkable illustrations of the *Gesa* will be found in ' Conary,' the noble poem of my friend, Sir Samuel Ferguson, who speaks of them as ' certain sacred injunctions, the violation of which was attended with temporal punishment.   The agents in inflicting such retribution appear in the form of Fairies.' (Poems by Sir Samuel Ferguson, p. 61. McGee, Dublin ; George Bell, London.)

Page 39. *Deirdré and he were playing chess together:*

Chess was a favourite game with the Irish, and is frequently alluded to in the earliest tales.

Page 73. *The 'Lia Fail,' and Ogham lore revered.*

The 'Lia Fail,' or 'Stone of Destiny,' was the stone on which the Irish 'Chief Kings,' or Ard-Righs, were crowned at Tara. It was subsequently used for the same purpose during many centuries in Scotland, to which it had been brought by the Dalriad Irish recorded by Bede, at the coronation of her Kings of Irish race. It was removed by Edward the First from Scone to Westminster Abbey, where it still supports the chair of Edward the Confessor. (See 'Hist. of Scotland' by Sir Walter Scott, vol. i. p. 34.)

Page 105. *Or Acaill;*

Now Achill Head.

Page 146. *Hail Eric just.*

The fine exacted for various offences by the Brehon law.

Page 151. *The dread Mor Reega.*

The War Goddess of the ancient Irish. An account of this divinity will be found in the admirable essay contributed to the 'Revue Celtique' (May 1870), by W. M. Hennessy, Esq.

Page 153. *Among the Sidils.*

The Fairy Hills.

Page 181. *There shone the torque of Meave.*

' Take off his armour that I may see the Brooch for the sake of which he undertook the combat. Leagh came, and stripped Ferdia. . . . . Cuchullain saw the brooch; and he began to lament and moan for him.' (MS. translation, by Professor O'Looney.)

Page 191. *An I, southward next, that lake.*

Lough Derg in Donegal, a place of pilgrimage still frequented. To this island properly belongs the legend illustrated by Calderon in his 'Purgatory of St. Patrick,' so admirably presented to the English reader by my lamented friend, the late Denis Florence MacCarthy.

Page 201. *Beside Ath-Luain.*

Now Athlone.

Page 226. *From Caiseal's crested rock.*

Now Cashel.

LONDON : PRINTED BY
SPOTTISWOODE AND CO., NEW-STREET SQUARE
AND PARLIAMENT STREET

R